DISCARD

D1482694

DISCARD

TWICE IN TIME

". . . whoever has sufficiently considered
the present state of things might certainly con-
clude as to both the future and the past."

Montaigne, BOOK II, CHAPTER 12

TWICE IN TIME

MANLY WADE WELLMAN

AVALON BOOKS

22 EAST 60TH STREET   NEW YORK 22

301 99635

PUBLISHED SIMULTANEOUSLY IN THE DOMINION OF CANADA
BY THE RYERSON PRESS, TORONTO

PRINTED IN THE UNITED STATES OF AMERICA
BY THE COLONIAL PRESS INC., CLINTON, MASSACHUSETTS

To

Richard McKenna

"Let every man be master of his time . . ."

CONTENTS

Foreword

The editors and publishers must make clear at once that they do not vouch for the truth of the unusual account here presented.

It came to their attention through friends of Father David Sutton, a Roman Catholic priest teaching classic languages at a parochial school in Nebraska. Father Sutton says that he visited Italy in 1947, and, while at the village of Bartolozzi, some miles north of Florence, he watched the clearing away of the wrecked church of San Marco di Giorno, which had been demolished by air bombardment during the summer of 1944. At that time, continues Father Sutton, one of the workmen, Antonio Paoli, brought him a tarnished silver casket, which Father Sutton bought for four American dollars. On the lid, which was welded or soldered shut, was deeply incised, in Latin, French and Italian:

Let no man open or dispose of this casket, on peril of his immortal soul, before April of 1957.

Father Sutton appears to have respected the injunction, and to have waited until May 21, 1957, before prying the casket open. It proved to contain a bundle of sheets of paper, written over in ink with small, close script in modern English, and bound with gold wire into the form of a rough book. Within an hour of beginning to read the manuscript, Father Sutton summoned several of his colleagues at the school, to help him determine whether or not his discovery was of importance. Scholars at DePaul University, the Catholic University of America, and Boston College became interested, and eventually both casket and manuscript were brought to New York.

The casket itself is of darkly corroded silver, and is shallow and rectangular, measuring approximately twelve inches by nine by three. Antiquarians generally agree that it is of simple but recognizable Italian Renaissance workmanship, probably no less than four hundred years old. The manuscript has occasioned dispute, some experts feeling assured of the great age of both paper and ink, others insisting that a clever forgery is possible and even probable.

Father Sutton's character as a completely honest and highly intelligent man is vouched for by many associates, both clergymen and laymen.

An effort to find Antonio Paoli has failed thus far. He is said to have joined the Communist Party of Italy, and to have gone to Hungary. There, according to investigators, he left the Communist Party in 1953, later became involved in the Hungarian resistance of the Russian-dominated government, and is believed to have been killed during street fighting in Budapest, late in 1956.

Considerable mystery surrounds the name of Leo

Thrasher, the purported author of the document. Dr. George D. Thrasher of Chicago, an engineer and nuclear physicist serving as consultant to a classified Federal project, says that his only son, Leon, disappeared in or near Florence in April, 1957. He adds that Leo Thrasher was only ten years old when the sealed casket came into Father Sutton's possession, and was in the fifth grade at a Chicago private primary school; at that time, his chief interest was in simple stories about interplanetary adventure. Dr. Thrasher insists that he cannot tell whether the handwriting of the document resembles that of his vanished son.

No better success has attended efforts to identify and locate George Astley, whose name appears early in the manuscript. It is understood that several creditors are eager to discover the whereabouts of one George Astley, formely of Atlanta, Georgia, who went to Italy in 1956. A recent report that he was living in Mexico, under the name of Gordon Jackson, cannot be substantiated.

Several passages in the manuscript, including a large one at the very beginning, have been classified by Federal agencies as not to be released for publication. What has been unclassified is here offered as an undeniable curiosity.

I. THE TIME REFLECTOR

"All right, all right," said George Astley again. "That's enough talk about time travel. How about showing me those flying saucers?"

"I didn't say I'd show you flying saucers," I reminded him. "I said I brought you up here because you believe in flying saucers."

"Oh, I believe in them." He sat down, fat and mystified. "So does Jackie Gleason. So do lots of other people. What's the connection with your gadget over there?"

We were in the sitting room of my suite at Tomasulo's Inn, on a hill above the Arno. It is my clearest memory of that time. Late April was chilly for Tuscany, and charcoal burned in the grate. My half-finished paintings stood stacked against a wall. Most of the room was cluttered with the metal scaffold I coupled together as I talked to George Astley.

"You say it's a time-traveling machine?" he prompted me. "Like the one in H. G. Wells?"

"Not a bit like the one in H. G. Wells," I assured him. "Wells wrote about a sort of century-jumping mechanical horse. You could ride it forward to Judgment Day or back to when the world was made. Mine doesn't carry you; it reflects you."

I lifted the heavy housing that held my carefully polished lens of alum, more than two feet in diameter. "Help me moor this in place," I invited.

"None for me, thanks." Astley turned his plump face toward the pier glass by the door. "Reflects you? Like a mirror?" He grimaced. "I won't go for this gag, Thrasher. Come on back to Florence with me. Let's have some drinks, and talk to a couple of girls I know. Tourists, college girls from Massachusetts. They want to meet a real live artist."

I shook my head. "No. The controls are set for a time-pattern involving today, this hour, and the five minutes and five seconds just about to come along. Anyway, I'm not an artist yet. Maybe sometime I'll be one."

"Past or future?" Astley grinned at me. "Give me that past-future routine again."

It was irksome to repeat explanations to someone who probably could not understand even if he wanted to, but I tried. "Past and future are the same time, if you think of time as a line of progression, instead of just a point."

"I've read enough of Einstein for that," growled Astley, who, I'm sure, had read only Sunday newspaper features about Einstein.

"Have you read *The Direction of Time*, by Hans Reichenbach? About the negative unit charge of the electron, traveling forward in time, while the charge of the positron charges backward?"

"No," said Astley. "And now that you've warned me, I won't. But I've heard you talk about the past as a backward trail, and the future as any number of forward trails."

"Only the *possible* future," I corrected. "The future, as it becomes present, extends the single trail forward from the past. Eventually, the future becomes the past. Today was yesterday's tomorrow."

"Don't be banal, Thrasher," begged Astley, whom I remember as banal to a painful degree. "So time's a single line, going forward and backward from here and now. That involves you, doesn't it? You have three space dimensions. You're six feet tall, say, eighteen inches wide and eight inches thick. And how many years deep are you?"

"Nineteen, going on twenty."

"Just the right age to know everything," taunted Astley, who was twenty-six. "And your time-shape is a line, a corridor. It starts wherever and whenever you were born—"

"Chicago," I supplied.

"It goes on from there, through America as you grew and traveled, and across the ocean here, to Tomasulo's just outside Florence. It will go on from here until you're dead and buried and stationary. It can't break off and start somewhere else. It can't double-track. All the science-fiction books argue themselves stupid about that. How do you argue that you can travel through time?"

"By being reflected." This, too, I had tried—and failed—to explain to him. I pointed to the lens, clamped into the heart of the machine's scaffolding. "Think of a burning glass, involving and transferring the power of light through space to another position."

"You said a mirror."

"No, *you* said a mirror. Or think of a TV projector, sending an image miles away—in this case, years away. Think of that image duplicated in that other time or place, in substance as well as appearance." I drew a long breath. "From Florence of 1957, say, to Florence four or five centuries ago, when things were at their greatest. Florence of the Renaissance, the Quattrocento."

"Come on to town with me." Astley showed uneasiness, which meant that he was beginning to take me seriously. "Come to the fencing academy. This is the day I can beat you, saber or foil. After that, we'll see those girls—"

"In Florence of the Renaissance," I broke him off, "I'll do something to prove I was there. Maybe paint a good picture."

"How did your father let you study painting, when he wanted you to get into nuclear physics?"

"He thought he'd let me learn the hard way that nobody today wants pictures by modern artists. Then I'd come into his project, as he tried to bring me up to do. But never mind that now. If I paint a mural that can't be destroyed without tearing the whole building down—then, coming back to this time, I could take you to look at the picture."

"That'll be the day," said Astley, lighting a cigarette.

"That'll be the day, indeed, and not far off. I don't seem to convince you."

He shook his head. "For convincing evidence, motive must be established."

"Motive?" I echoed him. "Look, Astley, would you take a voyage in a flying saucer if you were given a fifty-fifty chance of getting back alive?"

"Sure I would. I'd do it if I had only one chance in twenty of getting back alive. But I believe in flying saucers."

"Well, I believe in time-reflection. And I'm going."

"How will you get back? How do you get reflected, coming and going?"

"That's why I'm here at Tomasulo's. Look there at those notes on the side table."

He looked. "You've written down a date. '*April 30, 1470.*' And under that: '*Ceremony —rain prayer —ox on altar.*' "

"I've been digging through old records in the *Biblioteca Nazionale,* in town." I began to pull off my shoes. "Tomasulo's was a country house in 1470. A group of cultists gathered here on April 30, 1470

—just four hundred and thirteen years ago today."
I looked again at the time gauge on my camera control. "I'm set for that, exactly."

"Cultists?" Astley repeated a word he understood.

"Their contemporaries called them sorcerers and
Satanists," I told him. "Anyway, they were sacrificing
an ox on that day, trying to bring rain down on their
vineyards. The day must have been bright and sunny
—ideal for reflector work. The ox on the altar was
chemically the same substance as my body. My own
original molecules will disintegrate and scatter when
I'm reflected, but I'll be reflected yonder, in the year
1470."

"Your image?"

"Exactly duplicated," I insisted, "in appearance
and metabolism, in every organ and tissue and mole-
cule and impulse. Among other things, in every con-
volution and vibration of my brain. That means, in
my mind and awareness and personality and life."

I flung aside the rest of my clothes. "I'll go nude,
of course. I'm not sure of the reflection-transfer of
inanimate cloth or leather, or wood or metal."

"You've got it all fixed up, haven't you?" said Astley, still trying to believe I was bluffing. "How will
you fit into the Italian Renaissance, with your blue
eyes and butter-colored hair?"

"Many Fifteenth-Century Tuscans had blue eyes
and yellow hair," I said. "And I've studied archaic

Italian. I can speak their language, understand their idiom. I'll be all right."

He got to his feet, and at last he looked worried. "You're not messing me into this time gimmick, Thrasher."

I laughed and shook my head. "No, but you'll help. Tomorrow at this time, bring a fresh veal carcass—or a fat pig—here to this room. I'll rebuild my time reflector in Fifteenth-Century Florence, and reflect myself back to tell you all about it."

I switched on a light, then another. The machinery hummed; a great trembling glow came through the lens of alum, icy-blue, brilliant, full of tiny dancing motes.

"Listen, Thrasher," Astley began to plead, "this isn't like experimenting with rats or guinea pigs."

"I haven't experimented with rats or guinea pigs," I assured him, and glanced at my image in the pier glass. I looked tall, pink, lean but well-muscled, with a mop of wavy yellow hair. I stepped into the light from the lens. It felt chilly, and stealthy vibrations touched me.

"As a matter of fact," I elaborated, "I've never experimented with anything. You're about to witness the first operation of my time reflector on any living organism whatever."

"Your family—" Astley began to wail as I touched another switch beside the camera.

Intense white light flared around me; I felt weightless, helpless, as though a great wave had lifted me from my feet. The room faded swiftly —the walls, the windows, my stack of pictures, Astley beside the armchair. I was blind. I tasted pungency; my fibers sang and shook to a howling, bruising rhythm. There was a moment of incandescent pain, deafening noise, then blackness.

Afterward, there was exhausted peace, relaxation. My feet were aware of solid, level standing room; I saw another ghost of a scene, something with human figures in it, growing plainer, taking on color. Voices chattered together. Life, reality, came back.

And one voice suddenly dominated the others, speaking in resonant, understandable Italian:

"The miracle has come!"

II. THE FIRST HALF HOUR

Faces turned upward to look at me in round-eyed fascination. And all this was happening in the back yard of Tomasulo's Inn. It was a changed back yard, dominated by a simpler, newer building; but I recognized it in a drowsy, blurred way, as in semi-slumber.

My memory seemed to be lagging as I looked for flagstones and the clutter of innkeeper's jetsam. They were gone; a level stretch of turf was there, hedged with tall, close bushes of greenery. I stood in the center of this, on a platform or pedestal of cut and mortared stone.

Oh, I reminded myself, *the altar of the cult that sacrificed the ox.* I had read of it in the Twentieth Century, but that seemed like a childhood memory instead of study short days ago.

"Kneel," intoned the same voice that had hailed a miracle.

The watchers before me dropped humbly down. There were a dozen or so, of both sexes, most of them shabbily dressed. The men wore drab, faded blouses and smocks, with patched hose on their legs; and the women were untidily tricked out in full skirts, bodices, coifs or caps. Men and women alike had long hair, and several were as blond as myself.

Their faces bowed away from staring at me. They took me for something to be respected, feared. I felt that I had an advantage, and sprang lightly down from the altar.

"Rise up," I bade them, in my best Italian. "Who is chief among you?"

Slowly they came to their feet, and the tallest of them moved forward. "I am master of this coven," he murmured, watching me narrowly. "What is your will?"

"First of all, lend me that red cloak you wear."

He unclasped it from about his throat, and I draped it over myself.

"Now hark you all," I said to them. "Did you worship here because you sought a miraculous gift from heaven?"

"Not from heaven, exactly," said the man who had lent me his cloak.

He was the best clad of the party, in plum-colored hose and a black velvet surcoat that fell to his knees. His narrow waist —he was an inch taller than I, and as gaunt as a rake —was clasped by a leather belt with a round silver buckle, and at his hip swung a sheathed dagger. A red beard tufted his chin, and above this jutted a fine-cut long nose. His eyes were large and deep, the wisest eyes I had ever seen, and just then the most curiously intent. The hair receded thinly from his broad-domed brow.

Something about him suggested Shakespeare—Shakespeare's face, that is, more alert and enigmatic than generally pictured, set upon the body of Ichabod Crane.

"Not from heaven," he said again. "Rather from —our Father in the Lowest." He gestured downward with a large but graceful hand. "Why do you ask? Are you not come from him?"

I made haste to simulate a grasp of the situation, as I struggled to remember what I had read of this very incident—the prayers of a sorcerers' cult for rain, on April 30 of the year 1470.

"I am sent to be your friend," I announced solemnly. "This ox which you have offered—"

As I pointed toward the altar, I saw that the stones were bare, save for a slight dark moisture. I paused, then went on: "This ox which you have offered has been transmuted into me, that I may be your friend and guest and helper."

There was more truth in that than my velvet-coated interrogator could grasp, I told myself; but I did not know him as yet.

"Doubt not but that the rain will come," I added, with some assurance; on the horizon beyond the hedge, I saw a lifting bank of cloud.

"Thank you, messenger," breathed an elderly cult-ist at my side.

"Thank you, thank you," prayerfully echoed the others.

The lean spokesman in velvet bowed slightly, but I discerned a hint of growing laughter in those deep, sharp eyes. "Your visit is far more than we poor worshippers had presumed to expect," he said silkily. "Will you suffer these poor servants of yours to depart? And will you come to my humble dwelling yonder?"

I nodded agreement, and he gestured to the others in dismissal. They retired through a gap in the hedge, respectfully, but not with all the rapt wonder that such an apparent miracle might be thought to inspire. I felt surprised and a trifle disappointed; then I reflected that here, in the Fifteenth Century, people were more credulous. Coming to the ceremony in expectation of prodigies, they were not stunned when their expectations were fulfilled. I was strange, but I was not unbelievable.

"Come," invited the gaunt man, and I faced him.

I have compared his body to that of Ichabod Crane, but he was surer of his movements than the schoolmaster of Sleepy Hollow. Indeed, he seemed almost elegant just then, with his feet planted wide and one big hand bracketed upon his hip above the dagger.

"How are you called?" I asked him.

"My name is Guaracco," he replied. "The master of the coven which has just done worship here. But, if truly you are a messenger from him we delight to serve, why do you not know these things without my telling?"

A spice of mockery was in his tone, and I felt that I had best establish my defenses.

"Ser Guaracco," I addressed him bleakly, "you will do well to mind your manners. I did not come to be doubted."

"Oh, assuredly you did not," he agreed, but with a sort of triumphant amusement that made me uneasy. "Once more, will you come in with me?"

Another of his graceful gestures, toward the back door of the stone house that I knew for Tomasulo's Inn —for what one day would be Tomasulo's Inn. Walking with him across the turf, I pondered the matter. *What one day would be Tomasulo's Inn . . .* I must follow a new procession of thought, one that traveled two ways at once, from the past and also four centuries and more from the future.

To my mind came a fragment of conversation from *Through the Looking-Glass:* "It's a poor sort of memory that only works backwards." The White Queen had said that to Alice, and then: "Sometimes I've believed as many as six impossible things before breakfast." I reflected further on Lewis Carroll's mathematical mind, but Lewis Carroll, too, seemed dim and far off.

My new acquaintance stepped ahead of me as we walked, and tapped softly on the door. It opened at once. Upon the threshold stood a tiny male creature in a dark gown. He was no larger than a child of eight, and the bright face upturned to us might have seemed sweet if its shrewdness had not reminded me of Guaracco.

"Is this your son?" I asked.

Guaracco laughed quietly. "Yes, Ambassador from the Lowest. In some degree this is my son."

The little figure stood aside and let us enter a dark, narrow corridor. Guaracco's hand took my elbow through the folds of the borrowed cloak, and I allowed myself to be guided down the passage and into a room beyond.

Here were dark hangings, a thick carpet, chairs, a settee, and a table on which lay some bulky and ancient-seeming books. A single fat candle in a bronze sconce illuminated the room, for there was no window—only a barred air hole in the ceiling. Guaracco motioned me toward the settee.

"Give me leave to call for refreshment," he said, and clapped his hands.

From behind the draperies darted a figure as small as the one that had admitted us to the house. This one was hunched and misshapen, with a pinched face above the loose collar of a black gown, a face that looked old and bitter. Two long, knob-knuckled hands held a tray, with a silver flagon and two goblets of blue glass. Setting this on the table, the small figure backed out of sight again. I had not been able to judge sex or age in the brief moment of its presence.

Carefully Guaracco poured red wine from the flagon. "You do not ask," he said smoothly, "if that was another of my sons."

I did not reply. My memory, instead of growing clearer, seemed to become more scrambled; it worried me, and there was a definite feeling of menace in that shadowy room.

Guaracco lifted one of the goblets toward me. "He is as much my son as the other," he added. "Here, Ambassador, take this wine. I'll wager you'll never drink another draught like it."

I took the goblet, and he raised the other.

"A toast." His voice rang out, suddenly bitter. "Sir, your immediate transportation to the floor of hell, from which you lyingly came to be sent!"

I set down the goblet on the table and rose quickly, my fist doubled.

"Ser Guaracco," I said harshly, "I have had enough of your discourtesy. You doubt my being of another world, even when you saw me rise from the very substance of the ox—"

"Enough of that falsehood," he interrupted. "It was a trick."

Quickly he set his goblet beside mine, and again struck his palms together, twice. From the entrance to the passage darted the pretty little keeper of the door. From behind the hangings sprang the hideously withered bringer of wine. Each held a long, thin blade, curved like a scimitar and plainly of a whetted keenness.

Guaracco laughed calmly, as one who makes the winning move in a game. "Before my familiars cut you into ounces, you'd best confess your motives."

"Confess?" I blurted out.

"Aye, that. Oh, miracles have happened upon that altar ere this; but it was I, Guaracco, who taxed my brain and my machine shop to prepare them."

My mouth must have dropped foolishly open. Again he laughed.

"You come without my leave or knowledge. I do not brook rivals for my power, even where it concerns but those few foolish witch-worshippers. Out with your story, impostor, and do not lie more than you can help."

III. THE SERVICE OF GUARACCO

I cannot but be ashamed of the way I wilted. I might have faced out the surprise alone; the danger alone I might have braved. Together, they overwhelmed me.

Then and there, with Guaracco's fine teeth gleaming at me through his red beard, and the two dwarfs —who no longer seemed like little children—standing with ready swords, I told the truth, as briefly and simply as I could manage.

Guaracco listened with close attention, interrupting only to ask questions, and these were most intelligent questions indeed. When I had finished my story, he looked at me more penetratingly than before. At last he nodded, slowly and gravely.

"You will refuse to believe—" I started to sum up.

"But I do believe," he interrupted, in a voice surprisingly gentle. "I believe, lad, and in part I understand."

It was my turn to stare, but he did not mock me now.

"My understanding will be made perfect," he added, "when you and I have discussed this business more fully."

He snapped his big fingers at the dwarfs, and they

lowered their swords. With a jerk of his head, he dismissed them from the room. At once there was less menace in that candle-lit atmosphere; I felt relieved, and thirsty. But when I put out my hand for the goblet, Guaracco snatched it and spilled its contents upon the carpet.

"That draught was poisoned," he informed me, in the most casual of tones. "I meant to destroy you, as a spy or rival." He filled the goblet again. "Now, we shall drink to our better understanding."

We touched cups and drank. Guaracco's eyes above the brim were as knowing as Satan's own, and for the first time I was sure of their color —deep violet-blue, like ripe grapes.

"Come, this is better," I ventured, and smiled at him.

Guaracco did not smile back. "Never think," he said, his voice cold again, "that I cannot kill you later, if such course recommends itself to me. Those little entities you saw, frail though they appear, are half-parcels of doom. They handle their blades like bravos of thrice their size. They scale the tallest towers or wriggle through the narrowest openings, to deal death at my will. The skulls of their victims, destroyed in my service, would pave all the streets in Florence."

He stepped around the table and thrust his face close to mine. "Nor are they my only weapons. Your life could have been taken in half a score of ways between the yard and here, to say nothing of the

poison and steel I have seen fit to show you. Therefore sit down again, and hear my plans for you."

I sat down, with an unheroic show of acquiescence.
His teeth flashed in a grin of relish. "I seek power,"
he told me. "Much power is mine already. I wield
it, for instance, through the coven of deluded witch-
believers you saw, and through my spies and creatures
in the guilds and companies and councils. Also
through my influence with many individual persons,
base and noble, in Florence and elsewhere. My power
shall grow. One day I need not fear," his narrow chest
expanded a trifle, "to command Lorenzo himself."

"Lorenzo *il Magnifico* —the Magnificent," I murmured. "He rules in Florence, to be sure."

"He is prince in all but the name. But his time of
absolute rule, as I dare predict, will not continue
forever." Guaracco strode across the room, hands behind his back, then turned and faced me. "Hark you,
man from the future. You have said strange things
of the world from which you come. Yet they are not
such strange things, nor such great things, as are beyond my wish and strength to understand."

Gazing at him, I believed; he seemed to bristle
with wisdom.

"You will have sciences and devices to show me,"
he went on. "Machines, secrets, foreknowledges of
many valuable kinds. For them, I have spared your
life. You may yet be a chief among the agents in my
service."

He told me that with the flattest of assurance, and I did not have the resolution to challenge him. All that I could manage was my amazement that a sorcerer would be so interested in honest science.

"Ha, but sorcerers *are* scientists," he snapped out. "The simple folk gape at our learning as at a miracle of demons. To impress them, we mouth spells and flurry gestures. But the miracles are science, sane and practical. Do you deny that?"

I knew that I dared not deny it.

"If I am a sorcerer, so was Albertus Magnus. So was Roger Bacon, the English monk who gave us gunpowder. Or Berthold Schwartz, the German monk. And I may be as great as they. Aye, greater."

History, I found time to ponder, showed the wisdom and truth of what he said. Magic always foreran science; from alchemy's hocus-pocus had risen chemistry, physics and medicine. The quibblings of astrologers had made astronomy a great and exact field of study. And could not psychoanalysts look back to the ancient Chaldean magicians who sought to interpret the troubled dreams of Nebuchadnezzar?

But again I was trying to think in the future from which I had stepped, to think of things that had happened in the future. As before I attempted—and as before I failed—to rationalize the paradox of remembering things to come. Clouds darkened my mind.

"This traveling in time you have accomplished," continued Guaracco, tramping back and forth. "It is possible that we will attempt it together. Dearly would I love to see that world of which you speak, those ages that are to come." Again he paused in his nervous pacing, and leaned above me. "Tell me of weapons of war in that future time."

Slowly and vaguely, like a sick man, I tried to explain the breech-loading rifle, the machine gun, the tank. My explanations were faulty and imperfect, yet he listened and nodded eagerly. From a box on the table, he brought forth tablets and a red-leaded pencil with which to make diagrams of what I told him.

Guaracco drew crudely, and I took the pencil from him to improve his sketches. He tweaked the point of his foxy beard as he watched.

"By Mercury, the god of thieves, you truly are a reflection of what you were. Or is it by nature that you use your left hand instead of your right?"

"I am right-handed," I replied, but looked and saw that I had picked up the pencil in my left hand.

"Why then do you draw thus? Do you write also with your left? Show me."

I obeyed, with a few words, and his eyebrows shot up.

"That writing is backward, as some Oriental nations make their letters. What language is it? No, you write Italian, but it would take a mirror to read it."

Again he was right; I had not realized that I wrote

from right to left, and with my left hand. I made a woeful face over the problem, and he chuckled at me.

"You speak of a reflection, as by a mirror or a lens. And in a mirror, your image shows its left hand to be your right, and its right your left. That clinches the truth of what you claim."

I let the weird realization creep into my mind. Some time long ago—or long in the years to come—a man named Astley had mentioned the writings of another man named Wells. And Wells had told of someone called Plattner, who, venturing into strange dimensions, came back with his left hand skilled instead of his right.

I tried again with the pencil, and with some difficulty scrawled out my name as it should be read, from the left side of the page.

"Leo," read Guaracco aloud. "Leo Th— Trassi —a strange name, Ser Leo." Again he studied my sketches. "You depict things well. You have studied the arts? I thought so." Again a tweak at his beard. "I grow inspired concerning you."

"How?"

"We will go into the city of Florence. I shall introduce you as a kinsman of mine, newly from the country, who seeks to enroll in the ancient guild of Florentine painters. I know a fitting master, Messer Andrea del Verrocchio. I shall pay his fee to enter you as a student in his *bottega*."

"I shall study there?"

"You shall serve me there, or through there in other places. Verrocchio is well known and well liked. Great nobles patronize him. And I have not yet a proper agent among the arts. Perhaps you will suit nicely in that position. You agree?"

I bowed my head in acceptance, because there was nothing for me to do but accept. Guaracco actually patted my shoulder. "You will find us doing famously as adopted cousins, Leo."

Crossing the floor, he twitched back the hangings and opened a door to another room. I could see a bed and a cupboard within.

"You will rest here tonight," he informed me. "Come."

As I joined him, he led me inside and opened the cupboard. "Here may be some clothing that will fit you. We are of a height, we two, and not too dissimilar in girth." He handed me garments.

His hose stretched drum-tight upon my more muscular legs, and his doublet proved too narrow in shoulder and chest.

"That must be altered," he decided, and, going to the door, raised his voice. "Lisa!"

"My lord?" replied a soft voice from somewhere in another room.

"Come here, child, and bring your sewing tackle." He turned back to me. "Now, Leo—that is the name of the lion, and it matches well with your tawny mane—now you shall see what I count my greatest treasure."

As we came back to the larger room, a girl stepped through the door from the passage.

Not tall, but of a full and fine figure and graceful as a dancer, she paused on the threshold at sight of me. In her oval face were set large, soft eyes of deepest blue, and a shy, close-held little mouth that was so darkly red as to be nearly purple against the ivory pallor of her skin. Her thick, soot-black hair was combed as snug as a helmet, and caught into a bun at her neck. She wore a chemise of sober brown with a tight black bodice accentuating the rondure of her young bosom, and a full black skirt hid her feet. In her slim hands she held a flat iron box, the sewing kit Guaracco had commanded.

"Is she not beautiful?" Guaracco purred under his breath to me.

Beautiful indeed she was, but I did not feel like saying so to him.

"Lisa," he addressed her, "I present to you Messer Leo, a new associate of mine. He will be of value to us all; therefore be courteous to him. Begin by altering this doublet to his measure. Rip the seams here and here, and sew them again in a fuller manner."

Again he turned his gaze on me. "Leo, this girl is for you a model of obedience and singlehearted service." He might have spoken of a fine piece of furniture. "I bought her of her beggarly parents, eighteen years gone. She was no more than six months old, and since that time I have been father and mother and teacher to her. She knows no other lord than myself, no other motive than mine."

The girl bowed her head, as though embarrassed, and busied herself with scissors and needle. I sat down, Guaracco's red cloak still pulled around my naked shoulders.

"That bright mantle becomes you," Guaracco said to me. "Take it as a present from me. But we speak of Lisa. I trust her as I trust few."

He paused, but I offered no comment.

"She and the two imps you have seen," continued Guaracco, "are the closest to me of all my unorthodox household. Lisa cooks for me, sews for me, keeps this house for me. I, for my part, shelter and instruct her. Some day, for both our gains, I may give her to a new master —to some great lord, who will thank me for a handsome, submissive present."

It occurred to me then that such transactions were common in Renaissance times, but I disliked thinking of the gentle, lovely girl being so bestowed.

"She will cherish that great lord," wound up Guaracco, "and learn his secrets for me. Is that not true, Lisa?"

Lisa bowed her head still lower, and her ivory cheeks showed pink, like the sky at morning's first touch. I felt embarrassment and resentment on her behalf, but Guaracco laughed quietly and poured himself a half-goblet of wine. This he drank slowly, without inviting either of us to join him.

In a surprisingly short time, Lisa had finished broadening the doublet for me, and it fitted my torso like wax.

As evening drew near, we three took a meal in the hedged yard where Guaracco's dupes had prayed to infernal powers for rain. Whether by their prayers or by coincidence, rain did arrive, not long after we had finished the bread, chicken and salad that Lisa set before us. As the first drops fell, we went indoors and had wine and fresh peaches and honey for our dessert, in a great front room that was comfortably furnished with gilded couches and tapestries.

After the supper, Guaracco conducted me to his workshop, a large flag-floored cellar. Here was a bench, with lamps, retorts and labeled flasks for chemical experimentation; and in this branch of science I was to find my host—or captor—amazingly learned. The greater part of the space, however, was filled with tools and odds and ends of wooden and metal machinery.

At Guaracco's command, I tried to illustrate my scientific explanations with some of these, but my strangely blurred memory, like a partial amnesia, deceived me again. I made only the most slovenly demonstrations, and failed also to explain.

"You cannot be blamed for vagueness," said Guaracco, almost comfortingly. "A drop backward through so much time—four centuries and more—must surely shock one's sensibility."

"I seem to progress in generalities only," I complained.

"Even so, you are better grounded in such things than any man of this age," he encouraged me. "Talk more of that astounding power, electricity, and steam, too. I think I can see how it may work, like wind in a sail, or water on a mill wheel." His eyes brightened. "But stay. I have an inspiration."

He opened a small casket on the bench and fetched out a little bag of dark velvet. From this he tumbled a great rosy pearl, the size of a walnut and glowing as though with its own light. He caught it upon his open palm and thrust it under my nose.

"Look," he commanded.

To be sure, it must have been a priceless jewel, filled with rose and silver radiances like a sunset sky. It captivated me with the sudden impact of its beauty.

"Look," repeated Guaracco, and I looked, with eyes that seemed bound in their focus, at the pearl that grew bigger and brighter.

"Look," I heard him say yet again, as from a distance.

The light faded and consciousness dropped from me like a garment. I knew dim silence, as of sleep, then a slow return to my senses. I shook myself and yawned. And Guaracco laughed, his foxy face close to mine.

"How long did I sleep?" I asked, but he did not reply at once. Polishing the pearl upon his sleeve, he slid it carefully into his velvet bag.

"Some, if not all, of those forgotten things are buried in your mind. They can be recovered from their tomb. With you, I tried a way that fools call black magic."

Hypnotism, that was it. Perhaps he had truly drawn from my subconscious some of those technical matters that I seemed to have lost.

"Each minute of your company," he elaborated, "convinces me that I did well to spare your life. Now, draw for me again."

I obeyed, and he watched. Again he praised me, and swore that I would be placed as a student with Andrea del Verrocchio the very next day. It grew late, and he escorted me to my bedchamber, bidding me a cordial good night.

But when the door closed behind him, I heard a key turn in the heavy bronze lock.

IV. A STUDENT IN FLORENCE

On the following day torrents of rain fell, and the trip
to Florence was postponed. To my chagrin, the
clouded memories of various details of my Twentieth-
Century life had become even cloudier, so much
more so that I spent the morning making notes of
what remained to me. It gave me practice in writing
naturally instead of backward.

These notes Guaracco scanned, then appropriated,
with thanks as cordial as though I had done them
expressly for him. Near at hand, all this time, loitered
the uglier of his two dwarfs. There may have been
greater menaces at the window behind me, or hidden
in the tapestry at my elbow.

And so I stopped writing, and talked instead to
Lisa, the lovely quiet girl who had altered my doublet. She was shyly friendly, and possessed of unfail-
ing good manners and charm. That morning she had
more needlework to do; I sat talking and listening,
fascinated by the deft play of her pale fingers. While
we were together, I, at least, felt less the sense of
being a prisoner and an underling.

The rain ceased by sunset, and early the next morning Guaracco unlocked my door to call out that we
would go to Florence immediately after breakfast. We

ate quickly, and went out into the pleasant early sunshine. Servants—Guaracco had several, in a nearby cottage—came, leading a fine white stallion for him and an ordinary bay for me.

As I mounted, I glanced toward the house. Lisa stood at the door; when she caught my eye, she lifted her hand, timidly and almost stealthily. It was like a benediction, and I regretted leaving her. Off we cantered along a hard-pounded clay road, with a groom on a mule behind us.

We had not far to ride to Florence. I found the valley of the Arno much as once I had known it in that maddeningly blurred time to come. It was green and bounded by hills, its banks sprinkled with villas, clusters of peasant huts, and suburbs, with the town in the middle.

Florence itself was smaller than I had seen it, and newer and lovelier. The town lay secure behind high, battlemented walls of stone, with the river running through. I saw the swell of the Duomo, second cathedral of all Christendom, great and rounded and pale like the moon descended to Earth; and around it, the towers of white mansions and palaces, and the cool green of garden trees.

We entered a gate full twenty-five feet wide by fifteen high. The tall lintel of brown stone bore a basrelief of St. Mark's lion, complete with wings and book, also several female figures which appeared to have tails.

Within the walls, the town shone all new and fresh. By the clean whiteness of the houses and their style of architecture, I judged that nearly all of medieval Florence had been razed to allow this new Renaissance capital of the Medici its full glory.

The streets for the most part were smoothly paved, or at least had good gutters and cobbles. Some of them, the side streets, looked too narrow even for one-way wagon traffic, and were shadowed by the projecting upper stories of the houses. In many places these upper stories jutted so far as to make covered ways for pedestrians on both sides. Here and there stood the enclosed mansions of nobles or wealthy merchants; at many crossings were spacious squares, with statues of saints or heroes.

Many folk were abroad, on foot or on horseback, but there were few wains and carts, and most of these primitively clumsy. Nearly all transportation was by donkey pannier, or by baskets on the shoulders of sturdy porters. The people seemed prosperous, and in most cases happy. I reminded myself that Florence of the Medici enjoyed a unique freedom, and was wont to boast of that enjoyment to less favored Milan and Venice.

At last, on Guaracco's signal, we reined in before a tall, barnlike structure of drab stone, fronting away from the brink of the green Arno. It was three stories high, pierced with many barred windows, and furnished with a double door of heavy wood.

"This is Verrocchio's *bottega*," said my guide as we dismounted, then caught my elbow as I moved toward the door. "Before you enter here, Leo, I have a thought to burn into you."

With his deep, penetrating eyes, his red beard and suddenly sinister expression, he might have sat for a traditional portrait of Judas. Again I knew fierce dislike and resentment for him.

"You would exact a vow of fealty from me?" I suggested. "Vows begin, Messer Guaracco, only when hope is dead."

"I extract no vows. I but remind you that if you betray me in word or deed, if you seek ever to hurt or hinder me—if, in short, you do not adhere to the service I have set you—I will see you die by a death from which devils would veil their faces."

"I do not fear you," I said, striving in my heart to make this the truth.

"Nor do I seek your fear, but only your comprehension. If I have that, let us go in."

The great front room of the academy was as large as a riding hall, with lofty ceiling beams and whitewashed walls. The windows, all set toward clear, open ground, gave light enough to paint by. In the corners were jumbled plaster molds, half-finished paintings on blanks, broken chairs, pots of paint, sheaves of brushes, and rolled parchments and canvases.

Three or four young men stopped their various tasks to gaze inquiringly. Students, I took these to be.

And from behind a counter-like bench near the doorway, a man rose to greet Guaracco.

"Give you good day, Messer Andrea," said my patron. "I bring you a likely pupil. This is my own cousin, Leo."

The master of the *bottega* fixed upon me spectacled eyes above a snub nose. He was a spidery little fellow of forty or so, clad in a dark gown like a priest's with ill-fitting, worn slippers on his flat feet. His hair was gray, his beardless face white and puffy. His finest features were his wise eyes and his slender hands.

Guaracco praised me suavely, and offered a parcel of my drawings. Andrea del Verrocchio carried these to the light and squinted his eyes above him. Adjusting his spectacles, he peered at me again.

"You draw well," he commented. "Drawing is the father of all the arts. Would you learn to paint?"

Gratefully I said that it was a high ambition with me.

"If you study here," he warned, "you must work as I devise."

"To devise is for the master," I said respectfully. "To execute is for the pupil."

"Well worded." He nodded, smiling. "Come and look at this picture."

I followed him across the room. A sizable sheet of wood hung there, fixed to a sort of scaffold with cords and pins. Upon it had been painted, but not finished, an oil of the baptism of Jesus. Some of the figures were executed with skill, but over one of them—a kneeling winged angel—I could but shake my head.

"You see a fault?" inquired Verrocchio beside me.

"The draperies, good master, are not properly done."

He smiled slowly. The students, too, gathered to look, and I felt their critical attention. Perhaps they had worked at the painting, and had failed.

"Do you think you can better them, boy?" suggested Verrocchio, in a tone of good-humored skepticism.

"It may be, sir," I said. "May I use these paints?"

As I stooped toward some pots and brushes beside the painting, I glimpsed Guaracco's face, set in an easy smile. He seemed to trust my skill, if not my loyalty.

"Drapery is a science worth close study," I said to the group as I mixed some colors upon a rectangular palette. "That part of the fold which is farthest from the ends where it is confined," and I pointed with my brush handle to the fringe of the angel's robe, "will return most closely to its original extended condition."

"Aye, learned doctor," chuckled a student, with a burlesque of reverent attention.

"Show us what you mean," invited Verrocchio.

"With your leave, I shall try."

I dashed on my paint. Here was an old skill that I had not lost, even with the brush in my left hand.

"Everything naturally desires to remain in its own state," I elaborated as I worked. "Drapery desires to lie flat. If it is caught into folds or creases, thus," and I executed a crumpled crease upon the angel's knee, "it is forced to quit this condition of flatness and obeys the law of this force in that part where it is most constrained."

I progressed to the hem.

"The part farthest away from such constraint," I went on, quite confident now, "you will find returning most nearly to its original state. That is to say, lying extended and full."

"You say truth, my son, and you paint truth, too," Verrocchio agreed warmly, and turned to Guaracco. "Your kinsman stays here as my pupil and helper. Ser Leo, go forward with that drapery. When you have finished, the picture can need no further improvement."

Gladly I worked away, caring little that my new fellow-students had ceased to deride and stood watching, jealously. Meanwhile, Guaracco's groom fetched in a bundle of clothing for me, and Guaracco himself gave me a purse of clinking coins.

"I have paid the charge for your education, cousin," he said to me. "Bide here, live and work here, and do me credit. Do not forget what I require from you, according to our recent conversation. As for me, I may shortly take a house in Florence, not far from this *bottega*. Again I say, bear in mind my hopes and wishes."

With this equivocal farewell, he strode away, the very picture of a kindly and helpful kinsman.

And so I became a pupil of Andrea del Verrocchio, reckoned the finest teacher of the arts in Florence. I found that the other students were not at all bad fellows, and several were quite adept at their work. They were disposed to like me, treating my strange ways as evidence of foreign upbringing.

I had a cell-like room, with pallet bed and table, and my own chest of art materials. I listened dutifully to Verrocchio's precepts, and under his tutelage prospered at many kinds of work.

His taste was for sculpture, and though I thought this less intellectual than painting—for it cannot represent the transparencies or elasticities of nature—I did not rebel at fashioning clay, stone and metal.

My first piece of finished work, a gold ornament for the King of Portugal, Verrocchio generously called splendid. He let me help him with the great bronze busts he was fashioning for the palace of the Medicis, and he let me paint, alone, a series of ornamental shields for a wealthy merchant.

In the evenings, and sometimes in the daytime when work was at a lull, we students were permitted to walk out along the streets. I could never weary myself with the sights and sounds and smells of Florence.

Happily my heart responded to the pageantry of the main thoroughfares. I looked at trains of laden beasts, processions of armed men going from one guard post to another, occasional rich chariots of the great or ostentatious, cavaliers on prancing horses, veiled ladies in mule-litters. More roughly picturesque were the guildsmen, the artisans, club-twirling apprentices, beggars, gaping peasants from the country. Occasionally a *condottiero*, a captain of mercenaries, swaggered past, slashed and dangerous, his long sword sheath hoisting up the hem of his cloak.

On the poorer, narrower streets we met hucksters and small traders with baskets and trays, and bevies of bright-eyed girls, on the lookout for romantic adventure. In the wider spaces were palaces to admire, and across the Arno the great, sculptured stone bridges. And there were pleasant taverns, where young students might get good wine and plenty for copper coins.

So went the month of May, 1470. Twice during that time, Guaracco called at the *bottega* to voice honeyed concern for the progress of his cousin. But, woven through such conversation, my inner ear distinguished the warning and insistence of his power over me.

Once he remarked that Lisa —"You remember our little Lisa, kinsman!"—had sent me her warm regards. I found myself heartily grateful for that message from the shy girl I had known so briefly; and I found myself wistfully reminiscent, too.

The first of June dawned bright and sultry hot. I was up betimes, putting final touches to improvement of the scaffolding which Verrocchio used as an easel for large pictures. As I fitted cords to pulleys and winches, a boy came in from the street, approached me, and said under his breath that he had a message.

"A message?" I demanded, looking up. "For whom?"

"For you, Messer Leo," said the little fellow. "I am desired to conduct you to a house in the next street."

Then I saw that it was no boy, but the handsome dwarf who once had opened Guaracco's door to me.

I asked Verrocchio to excuse me for a few moments, and followed the dwarf out into the bright sunlight.

"Is it Guaracco who has sent for me?" I asked, but he only smiled mysteriously, then trotted in front to guide me. We turned a corner and there, at the river's brink, was a small square dwelling house surrounded by a green garden.

"Go in, Messer Leo," the dwarf directed me, and ran around to the back, as nimble as a dog.

I pushed down the latch and went in. I found myself in a cool, dark hall, paneled in varnished wood.

On a leather-cushioned sofa sat Lisa. She wore a snug-fitting dress of white silk. Her feet she held close together under the hem of the skirt, and her hands lay clasped in her lap. About her whole attitude was an air of tense, embarrassed expectancy.

She looked up as I came in, and I thought that never had I seen eyes at once so soft and so brilliant. Then she dropped her gaze. When I spoke her name, she made no answer.

As I stepped toward her, I saw a pale oblong on a round center table. It was a folded paper, and written upon it were three large letters:

LEO

"Is this for me?" I asked Lisa, who only nodded and bowed her head.

"Your pardon," I requested, and took the letter and opened it.

It was brief and to the point:

My Dear Adopted Kinsman:

Thus far you have pleased me much, and I have high points of our mutual advantage from your endeavor. It pleases me to make you a present.

In the short time you were my guest in the country, you seemed to admire my ward, Lisa, and she, for her part, admired you. The inference is, of course, obvious.

Take her, therefore, and I wish you joy of each other.

This, from
Guaracco

V. THE GIFT

The reading of that letter had two effects, overwhelming and sudden, like the two reports of a double-barreled gun.

My first impulse was surprised gratitude and tingling joy. Why had I not realized that I loved Lisa? How could I have helped but love her from the first moment I saw her? . . . Then came my second reaction, the horrified knowledge of what Guaracco meant by such a bestowal.

I looked at her. "Madonna," I said shakily. "This letter. You know what it says?"

She looked up again, and the living rose deepened upon her ivory cheek.

"Lisa, it cannot be," I blurted out.

"Cannot?" she repeated, no louder than a sigh. It might have been protest; it might have been agreement.

I overcame an impulse to fall on my knees before her, like any melodramatic courtier of that unrestrained age and land.

"Lisa," I said again, desperately striving to choose my words, "first of all, suffer me to say that I am deeply stirred by the mere thought of winning you. Guaracco seems ready to give you to me, and you appear ready to consent." I saw the trembling of her soft red lips. "Lisa, I cannot accept you at his hands."

I sat down beside her. She looked me full in the face. Her brilliant eyes opened wide, as though she, too, began to comprehend.

I took her hand in mine. "That subtle wizard Guaracco," I went on bitterly, "tries to rule us both by fear, but he does not think he is quite successful. He apprehends that orders are orders to us until there comes the opportunity to disdain them. Therefore, he seeks to rule us by happiness."

Her fingers caught mine. They were cool and unsteady, but strong.

"Confess it, Lisa," I begged her. "For a moment you, too, would have welcomed my love, and would have given your own."

She showed me her sweet little smile, with unparted red lips, but then shyness drowned her again, and she made no answer.

"Do you see that we cannot?" I said earnestly. "It would be sweet, I know. For me, it would be blessed happiness. But —Guaracco's touch upon us for that —heaven forfend!"

"Eloquently said, my young kinsman."

That was Guaracco's voice. I sprang up and spun around, ready to strike him, but he was not there. Only his laughter, like the whinny of a very wise and wicked horse, came through the empty air.

"Do not strive against nothingness, Leo. And do

not torment Lisa. Look at her, Leo. She loves you, poor child, as you love her."

Such words made it impossible for me to look at Lisa, and therefore I looked the harder for Guaracco. His mockery came from the room's very center, and I stepped in that direction.

At once, he fell silent, but his final syllable echoed, almost in my ear. A cluster of lamps hung just above my head, moored to the ceiling by twisted cords. Among the cupped sconces I spied a little cone of metal, like a funnel.

I fear that I swore aloud, and then, with a single leap and grasp, I was upon those lamps, pulling with all my strength.

They broke away and fell crashing. Now I saw a copper tube that had been hidden among the cords. I tore it from its roots in the ceiling; it had led, I knew, to another tube that went to the lips of Guaracco.

Once again, Guaracco laughed, this time from behind me. Again I turned. A panel in the woodwork had swung outward and he stepped through, all black velvet and flaming spike of beard and white-toothed smile. "By my faith, you are a quick one," he said. "I have fooled many a wise old grandfather with that trick."

I set myself to spring at him.

"Nay," he warned me quickly. "Do no violence,

nothing that you would not have set down as your last act on earth."

His hand lifted. It held a pistol. I stared for a moment, half forgetting my rage at his meddlesome game with Lisa and me. Surely pistols were not invented so early . . .

"From you, I learned to make it," he said, as though he read my unspoken question. "It is short, but it throws a ball as hard and as deep as the longest arquebus in Christendom. Do not force me to shoot you, cousin."

"Shoot if you will! I have said to Lisa, and I say to you, that I will not be led by love any deeper into your hateful service."

He wagged his high, half-bald head, with a great show of melancholy. "Alas, Leo, you do great and undeserved wrong to Lisa and to me. Only this morning she was happy at the thought of going to you. It would have enchanted you to see her. She laughed—quietly, of course, but she laughed—and clapped her sweet little hands. She even scanned the marriage service, by way of rehearsal."

I looked at him, nerving myself to endure his jibes above the pistol muzzle.

"Ah, I think I understand," he said suddenly. "You do not think that a poor apprentice of the arts can support a wife and household." He held out his free hand to me, and smiled like any indulgent father.

"Distress yourself no more. I myself shall dower the bride, and that generously."

Even Lisa caught her breath in amazement and disgust. I started forward again, coming so close to Guaracco that I found the muzzle of the pistol digging into the pit of my stomach.

"Back," he ordered me. "Back, I say, and at once. There, that is better. And what fantastic objection do you raise now?"

"You add money to beauty and love in the effort to buy me!" I accused him. "Dowry, a bribe to marriage —oh, you are infamous! Surely we live in the last days of the world!"

"Oh, not yet," he objected drily. "Not by four and a half centuries at the least, as you seem to forget."

I flung wide my arms, as though to invite a shot. "Kill me," I dared him. "You said once that you would kill me if I should disobey you. Well, I disobey. With my last breath I name you a sorry scoundrel, and certain meat for hell."

For one instant his nostrils flared; his eyes blazed bright and hard. Then he shook his head, and moved away from me, around the table.

"Perhaps the fault was mine, after all," he said, as one who concedes a point for the sake of argument. "I was too abrupt, Leo, for your dainty taste." He glanced aside, to where Lisa sat. "Forgive this ungallant fellow, my child. Perhaps another time—"

"There will be no other time for your sport with us," I broke in stubbornly.

He frowned. "Go back to Verrocchio, then. You have disappointed me, and you have shamed Lisa." He held up his free hand to check my further utterance. "Return to your labors among the arts, and let them cool your heart so that we may talk sensibly. Go."

I flung out of the house, and my blood was more fiery hot than the climbing sun overhead. Guaracco was right. I had shamed Lisa. Truly she had been ready to accept me. Even if this betokened Guaracco's hypnotic suggestion, she had been ready; she had hoped to hear my praises and pledges, to stand with me before a priest.

And had I been kind or comforting? Could I not have said, more plainly, that it was in reality Guaracco I refused, but that on some happier occasion . . . I snorted to myself as I strode along. Like many a man leaving a stormy scene, I was painfully aware of things I should have said and done.

And I loved Lisa.

There was no escape from that, even when I tried again to persuade myself that it was all Guaracco's adroit suggestion, that he may have hypnotized me as well as Lisa, from the first day he had brought us together. I loved her. And undoubtedly I had lost her.

As I approached the door of the *bottega,* a final

glow of rage swelled through me. I yearned to strike
Guaracco, to throttle him—or to set upon some other
enemy. A mood that was rare in me made my heart
and body thirst for violence.

It was then that a handsome gray horse, cantering
along the street, trod on a loose cobble. It stumbled
and fell, and its rider flew headlong.

Pedestrians hurried from both curbs. I myself
sprang to help the sprawling man, but with a grunt
and an oath he gained his feet and caught the bridle
of his horse. It would not rise.

"Your beast is hurt," I said.

"Not this devil-begotten nag." He dragged at the
bridle, then kicked the animal's gray ribs with his
sharp-toed riding boot.

Harshness to animals has never set well with me
and, as I have said, I was still shaken by anger. I
shouted now, in loud and fierce protest. The man
turned upon me. He was squat and sturdy, with a
forked black beard and two square front teeth under
a short upper lip. Beneath his cloak of brown cloth
bobbed a long sword.

"Do not meddle between me and my horse!" he
snapped, and once more heaved at the bridle. The
horse struggled up at last, and the little crowd fell
away on all sides. The master laughed cruelly.

"Did I not say that he was unhurt? Body of Bacchus, it was his clumsy hoof that threw us, curse it

and him!" He clutched the bit of the poor beast, and struck it across the face with his riding whip.

"Stop that!" I shouted, and caught his arm.

He tried to pull loose, but I was stronger than he. Quitting his hold on the bridle, he cut at me with his whip. I struck him solidly, and felt my knuckles bark on those two front teeth. He staggered back, screaming an oath.

I would have struck again, perhaps felled him on the cobbles, but Andrea del Verrocchio himself, running from the *bottega,* threw his body in front of me. Meanwhile, the black-bearded man had whipped out his sword. Swearing in a bloodcurdling fashion, he struggled to throw off two peacemakers and get at me.

"Are you mad, boy?" Verrocchio panted in my ear. "That is Gido, the first swordsman of Lorenzo de' Medici's palace guard!"

VI. SWORDS BESIDE THE ARNO

When I say that I did not flinch at Verrocchio's warning, I do not call myself brave, only possessed with reckless anger. I flung forward, almost upon the point of Gido's flourishing sword. Then a saving ounce of wit returned to me.

My eye caught a gleam at the hip of one in the growing throng around us. I made a long leaping stride, and before the fellow knew I was there, I had snatched his long straight blade from its scabbard.

"Thank you, friend," I said hastily. "You shall have your steel back when I have settled matters with Ser Gido the ruffler."

Gido bellowed like a bull, cursing me by every holy Christian name, and by some that smacked of the classic Greek and Roman. But by now I had recovered my self-possession, enough to recognize my danger and face it. I thrust away Verrocchio's trembling hands, and interrupted Gido in the middle of a fresh storm of abuse.

"You talk too loudly for a fighting man," I said. "Come, I am no helpless horse or weaponless burgher. Let him go, you good people. He needs blood-letting to ease that hot humor."

"There shall be blood-letting and to spare!" Gido promised loudly.

Verrocchio pleaded that there be no brawl outside his front door, but Gido howled that there must be a back courtyard where we could cut each other's throats in private. And, with the crowd clamoring and pushing after us, to that back courtyard we went, through a little gate beside the *bottega*.

At the grassy brink of the Arno was a level space flagged with stones. The spectators jammed close against the wall of the house and its paling at the side, while my adversary and I confronted each other near the water.

Gido afforded me a quick, businesslike scrutiny that had in it something of relish —the sort of gaze that a carver might bestow upon a tender and savory roast. With a quick flirt of his left arm, he wound his cloak around his elbow to serve as buckler. "I'll teach you to defy your betters," he vowed.

"Teach on," I invited him. "Good pupils ever outshine their masters."

I was telling myself to be calm, ruthless and wide-awake, and not to fear the raw point. I had fenced a year at my university, and after that at an academy of arms in Twentieth-Century Florence, where I had consistently outshone opponents like George Astley. It seemed to me that here, at least, was one science that being reflected through time had not muddled in my head.

Gido fell on guard. "Fortune favors the right," he muttered, and his square front teeth gleamed at his own pun. Indeed, I held my own weapon in my left hand, and it came to me that left-handed fencers are supposed to have a certain advantage.

I made a quick, simple attack. It was no more than a feeling thrust, and Gido's blade shifted easily to sweep mine aside. At once I made a recovery, ready for his riposte.

The riposte did not come. Instead, this crack swordsman of the Medici guard tried to beat down my weapon and so get at my breast. I yielded a little before his pressure, disengaged, parried in turn, and dropped back. Another of his slashing assaults I only half-broke with my edge, and felt the delicate sting of his point on my left wrist.

"First blood!" yelled one of the watchers, and a little cheer went up for my enemy.

But I was not injured. As Gido pressed to follow his advantage, I parried cleanly. Immediately, while he was yet extended in his forward lunge and well within my reach, I sped my riposte. He flung up his cloak-swaddled arm barely in time, and through half a dozen thicknesses of the brown cloth my edge bit its way. Gido swore in pain; blood, wet and red, sprang out upon the fabric.

"He who bleeds last bleeds longest," I paraphrased, and slashed sweepingly. Gido had to spring all the way back to escape, and upon his face dawned an expression of worried mystification.

I was perplexed, too. Was this indeed the best swordsman in Florence? Gido had the look, and—with Verrocchio, at least—the reputation of a master fencer; yet he no more than held his own against my own amateurish skill. He had missed his first attack, and a moment afterward he had been foolishly open to my riposte.

Then, as our blades grated together anew, I found the answer in my own semi-fogged memory. *Riposte*, that was it—or, rather, the lack of riposte. The movement, the counterattack made when your opponent's thrust has been parried and he has not yet recovered, is in great measure an instinct. But, in these Renaissance times, it had not been rationalized, was not yet made a studied semi-reflex of swordplay. In fact, it came to me, no scientific treatment of the riposte in swordplay can be found in any manual of the exercise published before the late Seventeenth Century. Knowing the formal science of it, I had a tremendous advantage.

"Fight, you knave," I taunted Gido. "I'll cut you into flitches like a pig."

He thrust wildly, and again I warded. With a quick straightening of my arm, I touched him again before he could recover. My point snagged his bearded cheek, and a scarlet thread showed; this time, the onlookers cheered for me.

Gido retreated two paces. His face looked sick and plaintive. "He is a devil," he choked out. "He knows a secret thrust."

"I'll show you my secret, drive it to your cowardly heart," I promised, following him. "Fight, or I'll butcher you."

He tried to oppose me, then gave back, as before, from my menacing point. Now that his nerve was gone, he seemed barely able to hold up his sword.

"I cannot stand against you," he mumbled.

"Show him mercy!" I heard Verrocchio's pleading cry, and I half-lowered my guard.

At once, Gido struck; only a quick recovery saved my life. Then I yelled and sprang upon him. My first slash he managed to parry, my second almost mowed away his upflung left arm. He staggered to one side and tried unsuccessfully to hold off my long lunging thrust, but I got home deep between his ribs. Pulling himself free of the steel, he turned and ran like a boy caught stealing fruit, and I ran after him.

He gained the gate that led to the street and leaned for a moment upon it. Half a dozen of the onlookers barred my way, yammering for me to content myself with so much victory, but I struggled through their hands and after Gido.

He opened the gate, then fell heavily through it. As I reached the street, with the throng at my heels, I almost trod upon my adversary. He lay across the curb, his head in the gutter, his sword under him.

Blood gushed from his mouth and drenched his black beard. He had only life enough left to fumble a silver crucifix from his bosom and drag it to his lips. Then he dropped it and went limp.

The fight and the fury oozed out of me as I looked, for his was the first violent death I had ever witnessed. I looked around at the staring faces, and saw among them that of the man whose sword I had plucked away.

"Take back your weapon," I said to him, but he drew fearfully out of my reach.

Hoofs thundered on the cobblestones. The knot of people pressed themselves against the front of the *bottega*, and a little cloud of horsemen approached. A voice shouted commandingly, and there was a quick, orderly dismounting. An armored man stooped to gaze at the body.

"It is Gido," he grunted. "And slain."

"What?" demanded a voice from behind. "Gido slain, you say?"

Two richly dressed men had remained upon their superb horses. One sat his saddle almost above me. He was a dark, handsome youngster, no older than I, with abundant curls descending from under his plumed velvet cap to the shoulders of his plum-colored surcoat. His belt, gloves and boots were embroidered with massy gold. He stared down at Gido, at me, and at the bloody sword in my hand.

It was the other of the pair, leaning above the neck

of his horse just beyond, who had spoken. He, too, was young, and tall and sinewy, with harpies blazoned richly upon the breast of his tunic. His strong face, framed between sweeps of coarse black hair, had broad features of a supreme ugliness; at the right corner of his mouth was a wart. To me, his appearance suggested something I had seen in my other life, perhaps a painting or a statue.

"My peerless Gido!" he said again. "Dead in a brawl!"

Here upon me had ridden Lorenzo the Magnificent, absolute ruler of the city of Florence. Now the eyes of this young despot shifted to fasten upon me. Bright, deadly intent flared out of them, like fire from black flint. "Is that the assassin?" he demanded. "Arrest him!"

"I am no assassin, Your Magnificence. It was a fair fight."

But two guardsmen, in mail and leather, moved swiftly to my elbows. The iron gauntlet of one snatched away my sword. The other man caught my shoulder. "Silence," he growled in my ear. "Speak when you are spoken to."

Others of the party were busy questioning witnesses, who were many and noisy. Lorenzo de' Medici, after favoring me with another long, unfriendly look, picked up his reins. "Bring him," he ordered my captors.

"Can you ride?" I was asked, and when I nodded,

the gray horse of Gido was led forward. I mounted, and a man-at-arms caught the bridle reins in the crook of his arm. Another sidled his horse close against me.

"Come, you go to prison," he said. "If you but move as though you thought to escape, my sword will shed your tripes out upon the street."

VII. LORENZO THE MAGNIFICENT

Lorenzo and his handsome companion had already ridden on. His retinue followed, one man with Gido's limp body across his saddlebow. I brought up the rear on the gray, with my guards. Behind me, the crowd murmured and fidgeted; and in its midst Andrea del Verrocchio stared through his spectacles and drummed his nervous hands together.

We rode some two miles, I judge, making several turns, before our little procession entered a great paved yard before a white stone palace. Grooms appeared to lead away the horses of Lorenzo and his companion, and the guardsmen entrusted with me marched me around to the rear.

I was ushered through a small barred gate in a building behind, then along a hallway in which stood a sentry in breastplate and steel cap, poising a halberd. At a word from one of my guards, this man unlocked a heavy door. The small room inside showed a rough floor of flagstones, a stool, and a single iron-latticed window.

"Await here your judgment," someone bade me, and I was locked in.

I waited. There was nothing to do but think, and no thoughts but doleful ones.

Here, if I wanted to view my plight philosophically, was an end to my adventure through time, an end that would settle decisively in the negative the question of whether I left any recognizable record of my journey. My knowledge from another era, which had given me victory over the swordsman, had brought me disaster. Lorenzo de' Medici, the greatest man in Florence, had noticed me with deadly anger. That scion of an accomplished and unscrupulous race had the power of life and death in his city; and in my case it was almost certainly the power of death which he would exercise.

True, I had been drawn on first, had fought only in self-defense, but what judge would hear me? Lorenzo, who through me had lost a servant he valued. And what jury would ponder my case? No jury. Probably I would not be allowed to speak to justify myself. A nod, a word, and I would be hanged or beheaded, with nobody to question or to mourn . . .

Nobody to mourn? But what about Lisa? Would she even hear of it? I strove to put her from my mind.

As I mused thus, in a mood that grew blacker by the moment, a faint stirring sound at the window made me lift my eyes. A small, childlike face hung there, the face of Guaracco's deceptively handsome dwarf.

He cautioned me to silence with a tiny finger at his lips, then, wriggling like a snake, inserted his wisp of a body between the bars. A moment later he stood in front of me, smoothing the wrinkles of his little surcoat.

"What do you here?" I demanded.

"Whisper, I pray you," he begged. "By a vine I swung over the wall. In a bramble-tuft I lurked, while a sentry passed by. I bring a message from Messer Guaracco, your master and mine."

A faint hope wakened in me. Guaracco had boasted of wielding influence in the town; if indeed he valued me, he might exert himself to set me free. "Well?" I prompted.

"He desires me to say that hanging is an easy death and a swift."

"I am to be hanged, then?"

"Perhaps." The little head wagged wisely. "That is the punishment for brawlers and killers in hot blood. But there are other punishments for other crimes." He smiled up impudently. "A witch, for instance, a sorcerer, may be burned at the stake. By comparison, that is a dolorous end."

I grew ironic in my turn. "I read the riddle, imp. Guaracco is anxious that I make no claims of coming to him miraculously, that I say nothing of being nourished to assist him in his intrigues."

"They breed quick minds where you come from," said the dwarf.

"Quick enough to apprehend when one is forsaken by a coward. Go back. Tell Guaracco that I know his selfish fears, and that I choose to let him keep them for a space. I may involve him in my ruin, or I may not."

"Better to hang than to burn," said the little fellow, thrusting himself through the bars again. "You are warned. Be practical in season." He vanished.

Time wore on, and I felt hungry and thirsty. Finally, pushing my stool back so that I could lean in the corner of the cell, I dozed off.

A rough voice wakened me. "God's tooth, knave, you do slumber at the very lip of death. Rise and come with me. Lorenzo the Magnificent commands you."

I got to my feet and rubbed my eyes. Night had come, and I walked out of my dark cell toward a light held at the open door. Two men in steel-mounted leather waited, a bristle-bearded captain and a lanky halberdier.

Between them, I walked out and across an open court —it was a clear, starry night —and in through the rear door of the palace. A sentry challenged us in the arras-hung vestibule; then, at the bearded captain's reply, he waved us on through a curtained doorway.

The room into which we came was not spacious, but lofty, and lighted by no less than eight lamps on tables and brackets, or slung by gilded chains to the groined ceiling. The walls were frescoed with scenes and figures from Greek mythology, and a rich carpet hid the floor.

At a table of polished ebony, inlaid at the edges with ivory, sat Lorenzo de' Medici in a magnificent, gownlike houppelande of dove-gray silk, with fur at the neck and wrists. His ugly face was toward us. Beside him was stationed a scribe or secretary in a hooded robe, holding a quill pen in his fingers.

And standing before Lorenzo, with his back to me, was a long, spare man with a red pate. He could be none other than Guaracco. As we entered, he was speaking, in the earnest, plausible manner he could assume so well.

"Magnificence," he argued smoothly, "if to be related to the unhappy young man is a crime, I must plead guilty and hope for your mercy. It is true that I arranged for his education, as Messer Andrea del Verrocchio testified even now. But concerning this murdering of your servant, I must swear that I have no reaction save amazement and sorrow."

He was clearing his skirts of me, or at least trying to. Lorenzo leaned back in his square-made chair of state.

"I wonder, I wonder," the ruler of Florence almost crooned. His eyes probed Guaracco like sharp needles, and their regard, at least, could unsettle the nerves of the sorcerer-scientist. "It is possible that you assigned him to the murdering of Gido. . . . Ha, but here is the young rogue himself. He may tell us something of value."

The captain pushed me forward with his knuckles

in my back. Lorenzo's eyes met mine, and I returned him as steady a gaze as I could muster.

"Stand aside, Guaracco," ordered Lorenzo. "Now, young man, your name?"

"I am called Leo Thrasher, Your Magnificence."

"Leo —what?"

Lorenzo shook his craggy head over the sound of my surname, which all Italians have found difficult. The clerk, pen in hand, asked me to spell it out.

"A barbarous cognomen, which bespeaks the barbarous fellow," pronounced Lorenzo sententiously. "What defense do you offer?"

"Only that I did not murder your guardsman, Magnificence, but killed him in fair fight."

Guaracco, standing at one side, drew in his lips and shook his head at me, as though to counsel prudence. Lorenzo took several written sheets from beside his monkish companion.

"Others testify that you were the aggressor," he said coldly. "You struck Gido after he had fallen from his horse."

"He flogged the beast cruelly," I protested. "I used but my naked fist, and he drew his sword. As I say, I defended myself."

"Do not contradict His Magnificence," the clerk cautioned me sourly.

"And do not traduce the memory of poor dead Gido," added Lorenzo, raking me with his eyes. "I have lost a good servant in him."

I felt the sudden prod of inspiration. "It may be, Magnificence," I offered, "that I can supply his loss."

"How's that?" exclaimed Lorenzo, his black eyes growing narrow. "As a swordsman of my guard? But Gido was supreme. He conquered hundreds."

"I remind Your Magnificence that I conquered Gido," I said, despite Guaracco's quick gesture for prudence.

Lorenzo saw that signal, and turned in his chair. "How now, Guaracco, by the bones of the saints! I do begin to understand. You arranged that this cousin of yours might rise on his victim's dead shoulders, and be taken into my service as a choice blade. Then one day, being near me, and myself unsuspecting—"

"Nay!" cried Guaracco, unstrung. "As heaven is my judge, this is none of my doing."

Even in my peril, I gloated over Guaracco's terror. Again I made bold to speak. "If Your Magnificence does not trust me to guard you, I have yet other worthy accomplishments." I tried to marshal what latter-day science my memory still permitted me. "I can build bridges. I can make a gun that shoots many times. I can show how to destroy fortresses—"

"Can you, indeed?" broke in Lorenzo. "How came a youth by all this knowledge? More of Guaracco's doing, I make no doubt. He is whispered to be a sorcerer." Again his darting glance made Guaracco writhe like a grub on a pin. "Are you such another, young man? Death is severely visited upon sorcerers."

I recognized defeat. Lorenzo, it seemed, had determined to have my life. Exasperatedly I shrugged my
shoulders. "I shall not fatigue Your Magnificence
with further useless pleas. Call me wizard as well as
murderer, if such be your whim. I am neither, but as
well be hanged for a sheep as for a lamb."

The captain caught my elbow as though to drag
me away, but Lorenzo flung up a long white hand,
with a many-jeweled ring upon its forefinger.

"What did you say? Tell me that again."

"I said, 'As well be hanged for a sheep as for a
lamb,'" I repeated wearily.

"Hanged for a sheep as for a—" A grin came slowly,
as though it did not well know the way to that proud
and rugged face. And it made Lorenzo strangely
handsome.

"Neatly and bravely said, by Bacchus!" he cried
out. Then, to the clerk: "Write that down. Here we
have one talent that was never taught him by yonder
dull Guaracco."

I was stunned with amazement at the delight with
which he had repeated the cliché.

"It is but a saying, Magnificence," I said. "A handful of old words."

"Yet is the thought new, a new thing under the
sun. Say on, Leo the Witty. If you are an assassin set
to kill me, your tongue is as tempered as your sword."

He called the phrase new—and, of course, it was!
The Fifteenth Century had never heard it spoken

before. Every cliché must have been devastating in its time.

Thus reprieved, I groped in my mind for another saying. The works of William Shakespeare, a good century in the future, came to my rescue. "Since I am graciously permitted to plead my case once more, suffer me to remind Your Magnificence that the quality of mercy is not strained; it drops as the gentle rain from heaven upon the place beneath—"

"Excellent!" crowed Lorenzo happily. "Clerk, have you written it all?" And he smiled upon me, widely and winningly. "Young sir, you go free."

"Magnificence!" I gasped, overwhelmed with relief.

Of course, he could do that, too. Mercy could be his whim instead of disaster. He flourished his hand in dismissal. "Swordsmen I can buy at a ducat a dozen, but men of ready wit and tongue are scarce in these decayed times. Tomorrow you shall have a further audience. Give you good night, Ser Leo."

I bowed myself away, still scarcely crediting my happy reversal of fortune. But as I walked down the palace steps and through the gate, Guaracco fell into step beside me. Under his half-draped cloak I caught the outline of that pistol he had learned to make from me.

"I have no word for you," I told him. "I wash my hands of you, as you washed yours of me in there, when my life hung by a thread."

"I never pledged myself to you," he reminded me,

"nor did I demand a pledge from you —only obedience."

"I have refused you obedience!"

"That news would make Lisa sorrowful," he sighed, "perhaps in more ways than one."

I whirled toward him. "Would you punish her on my account?"

"Surely you will never force me to such an injustice, Leo. Instead, you will be generous enough to share your good luck. You have won favor from Lorenzo. When you appear before him tomorrow, you will go with the benefit of my advice and guidance, and you will be properly grateful therefor."

And thus I sank deeper than ever into his clutches.

VIII. THE COURT OF LORENZO

Perhaps it is odd, and again perhaps not so odd, that I remember no more of that particular walk through the streets of Florence, of my hot disgust at Guaracco's confident manner, of his insistence that I aid him. It is my fixed belief that, during our conversation, he found and took the opportunity to throw his hypnotic spell upon me. He could do that, almost as well as the best Twentieth-Century psychologist.

Probably, as we walked together all the long way to Verrocchio's *bottega*—I entranced and somnambulistic, he alert and persuasive—he planted deep in my dream-shackled mind the assurance that I was his friend and debtor, and that I must share Lorenzo's favor with him.

What I do remember is the next afternoon, and an equerry from the palace, bearing a message that summoned me to his master. I went, clad in my simple best —the decent doublet and hose which Guaracco had given me on my first evening at his country house, my red mantle, and a flat velvet cap with a heron's feather. The equerry had brought me a horse, the same fine gray over which I had fallen out with the lamented Gido.

"The beast is a present from His Magnificence," said the equerry as we mounted.

To the palace we rode. There, while my horse was taken by a groom to the stables, I was conducted through a great courtyard to a rich garden among high hedges of blocky-trimmed yew, with nichelike hollows for stone benches or white statues. There were roses, both on bushes and climbing briars; flowering shrubs in clumps and ordered rows; a perfectly round little pool with water lilies —all of this luxurious and lovely, though perhaps a trifle too formal. In the center of all this, under a striped awning, Lorenzo and his friends lounged at their ease on cushioned seats of gilded wood and leather.

To the four other guests I was introduced simply as Messer Leo; His Magnificence still shied at pronouncing my surname, which he found barbarous. I bowed to each of the others as his name was spoken. First there was Lorenzo's younger brother and co-despot Giuliano, the same cavalier who had ridden with Lorenzo upon me at the moment of Gido's death. Giuliano was one of the handsomest men I ever saw, even as Lorenzo was one of the ugliest.

Next in order came an elderly churchman with a fine, merry face and plain but rich vestments — Mariotto Arlotta, the aristocratic abbot of the woodland monastery of Camaldoli. His repartee was called the sharpest and quickest in all Tuscany, and indeed he jested in a lively fashion, not always ecclesiastical.

At the abbot's side sat a plump, courteous young man in his middle twenties—Sandro Botticelli, the rising court painter; I found him friendly, though moody.

The last of the group, and the youngest, was an adolescent poet, Agnolo Poliziano. Uglier even than Lorenzo, he was wry-necked, crooked-mouthed, beak-nosed and bandy-legged. Yet, for all his sorry person and raw youth, Poliziano was eloquent, thoroughly sophisticated and learned. From him I was to learn, in later days, much of what a man must know to shine in Florentine society under the Medici.

"A young sparkle-wit," Lorenzo said as he presented me. "For a time, I suspected that he had been thrown in my way to assassinate me. Yet am I drawn to him by the lustrant wisdom of his speech. 'As well hang me for a sheep as for a lamb,' he said to me yesterday." And he paused, to let the saying go around the instantly delighted group, from mouth to merry mouth.

"But even if he should prove dangerous," went on Lorenzo, "yet shall I keep him, even as I keep the lions at the Piazza del Signoria. Guard me, all of you, from any weapon save his tongue." He smiled at me. "Well, and what of your sorcerer cousin Guaracco?"

To my surprise, I found myself speaking earnestly and eloquently on Guaracco's behalf. It was as though I had been rehearsed . . . indeed, I realized suddenly as I spoke, probably I had been rehearsed, and by Guaracco himself. Hypnotists can do such things.

I fell silent in the middle of a sentence, unhappy at the thought that I had been used as a puppet and a parrot. But again Lorenzo smiled, and again seemed far less ugly. "By the mass, Ser Leo, I could wish that my own kinsmen spoke so well on my behalf. Your eloquence saved you yesterday; today it recommends Guaracco."

"I have been presumptuous, Magnificence," I apologized.

"Nay. I have thought him dull, but he does know something of science. You inspire me to send for him, for all he is a reputed wizard."

"Wizardry can never prevail against pure hearts," contributed Abbot Mariotta, at which all laughed rather heartily for so mild a pleasantry.

The equerry who had brought me was dispatched to find and bring Guaracco. Meanwhile, I was urged to sit down, and a demure but superbly proportioned maidservant, in the tightest of blue dresses, served wine to me. The conversation was then turning on the subject of a new alliance of the Italian city-states against possible Turkish invasion.

"This infidel threat comes in a happy hour," Lorenzo pronounced weightily. "Taunted and menaced, we Christians forget our own differences and draw together for our common safety. Thus the Sultan dares not attack us, we dare not quarrel among ourselves, and peace reigns."

"Your Magnificence does not like war, then?" I ventured.

He shook his ugly crag of a head. "No whit. War is expensive."

"And vulgar," added Botticelli.

"Aye, and unpredictably dangerous," chimed in the poet Poliziano.

"And in defiance of the will of heaven." The abbot crowned the matter.

"And yet," resumed Lorenzo, "it is well for a state to prepare for war, that others may fearfully continue to keep the peace. I have it in mind, Ser Leo, that you spoke yesterday of war engines, specifically of a gun that can shoot many times."

"Even so," was my reply, but at once I knew how poorly my scrambled memory might serve me.

"Some of Guaracco's witchcraft?"

"Not a grain," I protested quickly. "I have only honest science and mechanics in my devices, Your Magnificence."

All the while, I was trying to think of how a machine gun might be fashioned. I wished that I had mentioned some other weapon.

But Lorenzo told Poliziano to fetch paper and pencils, and ordered me to draw plans for such a gun at once. I made shift in some fashion to picture a gun carriage, with wheels and a trail, which mounted not one barrel but a row of ten.

"It is not of particular brilliance," drawled the poet, watching. "A rank of arquebusiers would serve as well."

"Aye, but what if we have not overmany ranks of arquebusiers?" countered Lorenzo, and again gave me a most generous smile. "A single man, I apprehend, could aim and fire this row of guns. Ten such machines would offer a full hundred shot. And, well aimed and timely discharged, that hundred shot might decide a great battle."

Encouraged, I sought to vary the principle. I drew a larger and wider carriage; this held not small barrels but heavier cannon, placed in a row and slightly slanted toward the center. Such a multiple piece of artillery, I argued, could be wheeled into position and the fuses lighted in quick succession; then it would throw a shower of shot against a single small area upon a wall or rampart, battering it down.

"You speak truly!" applauded Lorenzo. "It would outshine the greatest battering-ram in Christendom."

"And it could be improved further," I continued, more boldly, "by using explosive shot in the cannon."

"Explosive shot?" echoed Giuliano. "How is that, Ser Leo? Can you make lead and iron to explode?"

"Aye, that, with powder and a fuse inside," I said, though none too confidently.

"Nay," argued Giuliano. "Such a shot would then burst at the very mouth of the cannon, perhaps splitting its barrel and doing injury to our own soldiers."

I was forced to shake my head, saying that full explanations would prove long and wearisome for so pleasant an occasion.

"Then answer another time," said Lorenzo kindly. "Meanwhile," and he gathered up my drawings, "these shall go to my armorers, that they may make models for me."

"This young man draws well," contributed Botticelli. "He bears out the good reputation Verrocchio gives him."

Evening had drawn on. Silver and gold lamps were lighted, and servants brought us a rich and spicy supper in the garden. There was plenty of wine and all of us drank freely, not excepting the abbot. Finally fruits and ice-cooled sherbet were fetched to us; and at this dessert, we were joined by half a dozen ladies.

They were as beautiful, those ladies, as any in the Hollywood I had known in my other existence, and they were dressed to call attention to their beauty. They wore rich brocade and gleaming silk, fitted to each shapely body like a coat of varnish, cut audaciously low over ripe bosoms, narrow-skirted around graceful limbs. Jewels sparkled on caps and coifs, from bracelets and pendants and brooches.

And most arrestingly lovely among these was the famous Simonetta Vespucci, the reigning toast of Florence, here among us without her complacently dull husband. I judged that she was no older than I, but in body and manner she was delectably mature. Her shoulders sloped somewhat, and her neck was long; yet these did not detract from the ripe elegance of her tall figure, so frankly revealed to us by the flame-colored satin she wore. Her abundant hair gleamed more richly golden than the gold thread of the sapphire-jeweled net she wore upon it. Her proud face was at once warmly and purely exquisite, and her expression showed that she knew her power.

Every man there was her frank and devoted admirer. I had heard that the very shopkeepers and workmen who saw her passing along the street would roll their eyes in awe, would even fight jealously over this noble creature they dared not address. I could understand such a reputation. As for Simonetta herself, she dispensed smiles among us as she might have dispensed coins among beggars; and of us all, she plainly preferred the dark, dashing Giuliano de' Medici.

"I fear this summer will be hot," she mourned alluringly above her sherbet cup. "There will be little ice left in the storehouses by autumn."

"Nay, then," I said, "ice may be kept through the hottest of weather, if it is but placed in houses well banked with earth." I sketched such a half-buried shed quickly. "And also let the ice be covered deeply with sawdust and chaff."

"I have seen chaff placed by a farmer over his fruit, to keep it from freezing. If chaff keeps fruit warm, how will it make ice cold?" said Botticelli.

I forebore to talk about refrigeration and insulation, for it might prove boresomely incomprehensible to the company. "It does indeed bring coldness," I assured Botticelli, "or rather, it keeps the coldness that is already there."

"Nay, that smacks of black magic," said Abbot Mariotto, crossing himself with a beringed hand.

"Rather of white magic, good Father," suggested Lorenzo. "It helps men, does it not? And works harm to no creature. Ser Leo, do you guarantee that ice would thus remain unperished all through the summer?" He beckoned a servant. "Go you, and summon a secretary. He shall make notes of these things Ser Leo tells us, and tomorrow I shall see to the building of such a house. Therein my ice shall lie, with good store of chaff to preserve it."

"This strange young man looks like a cavalier, but speaks like a learned doctor," said one of the ladies, a bosomy dark creature in green, as she toyed with a goblet of jeweled gold. "But does he not know of more romantic matters than chaff and houses banked with earth?"

"Aye, Messer Leo," put in Simonetta, deigning to smile upon me. "Will you not speak to us, say, of

these little stars which do wink out in the sky above
our earth?"

Her eyes and her smile, brighter than the stars of
which she spoke, would have dazzled any man. Perhaps that is why I ventured to impress her.

"Madonna Simonetta, suffer me to say that those
stars are not small, but are worlds greater than our
sun."

"Say you so?" she cried, and laughed most musi-
cally. "But they are only twinklets, full of spikes and
beams like tiny bright burrs."

"They are far away, Madonna," I explained. "A
tall man, if only at the distance of a hundred paces,
appears so small to you that he seems to be contained
in the eye of a needle held up before you. So it is
with these bodies in the sky."

"But you said greater than the sun," she argued.
"The sun, Messer Leo, is round like a ball, not full
of points like a star."

I took up a sheet of the paper on which I had been
sketching, and asked for the loan of a pin. The lady
in green offered me a silver bodkin, and with this I
pierced a hole in the paper.

"Now, Madonna Simonetta," I directed, "hold this
hole to your eye, so that you may look through it.
The smallness of the opening serves to shut away the
glitter. So . . . you do it correctly. Now," and I
pointed to where shimmering Jupiter hung in the
evening sky, "look yonder at that bright star. Seen

through the hole in the paper, does it appear like a burr, or like a small round body?"

She peered. "This is a marvel!" she cried. "It is indeed round, like a golden coin seen from a distance."

The others rose to cluster around her, and each in turn must needs look through the hole in the paper at Jupiter. I turned over in my mind the possibility of explaining and diagraming a telescope, but again decided not to offer a foggy discourse that I could not support with exact plans or models. I contented myself with attempting a lecture on astronomy.

"Gentlemen and fair ladies," I said, as meaningfully as I could manage, "these stars look so small that nothing appears less; yet a great many are larger than our own Earth. Think how trivial our world would appear if—"

"Faith, cousin," called out a ringing voice I knew, "you seek to belittle this great wide world, and Florence, and Lorenzo the Magnificent."

It was Guaracco, absolutely overwhelming in blue and gold, who strode forward and made his respectful compliments all around.

"I pray you, Magnificence, forgive my young kinsman if he has been impertinent," he purred. Then, turning to me: "Will you step aside, Leo? I have a message for you from Lisa."

At mention of that name, Botticelli laughingly congratulated me on having a sweetheart, and I thought the lady in green pouted. Indeed, I felt a quickening of my pulse as Guaracco drew me by the elbow a little way from the group in the lamplight. "What is her message?" I asked him eagerly.

"That was but an excuse that I might speak to you alone and apart. Say no more of these matters of the stars."

"But why not?" I demanded, amazed.

"The stars in their courses are a special knowledge of sorcerers. I overheard your teaching just now."

"But I taught truth," I said hotly.

"Do I not know that? Do you dream that I think this little mote, our planet, is the center of all things?" Guaracco shook his head. "But the old belief is part of my trade. I frighten or reward or persuade men by horoscopes, and prophecies from the stars. Do not show me a liar, therefore; else I may smooth your way to destruction."

I glared back into his fierce eyes, but more in wonder than in rage. Once again Guaracco revealed himself a sound scientist; and once again he showed that he hid his knowledge, and fostered error, for his own profit.

I need not be too ashamed, I feel, to say that he made me afraid.

IX. THE END OF THE EVENING

Guaracco tried, intelligently and constructively, to be the lion of the occasion. He could charm and amaze and inform. Listening to him, Lorenzo publicly and good-humoredly withdrew his previous opinion that Guaracco was dull, and bade him talk on any subject it might please him to choose. Philosophical conversation, it seemed, intrigued Lorenzo, as the jokes and horseplay of a jester might intrigue a shallower-minded ruler.

Guaracco obliged, by offering sage improvements upon my specifications for war machines. He spoke knowledgeably of armored vehicles, ships that could dive, and—more specifically and practically—of an improvement for the crossbows of Lorenzo's guard, a simple, swift-working lever to draw and set the bow-string, instead of the slower crank mechanism.

I realized that I had spoken of just such a device to Guaracco on our first evening together. Piqued, I heard the company's praise and approval of the lever, and watched Guaracco beam back at Lorenzo and the others as he accepted the commendation for himself. He tried to draw an explanatory diagram, but was clumsy. On an impulse that was not exactly large-hearted, I stepped forward, twitched the pencil out of his hand, and made the sketch myself.

"Do you not also admire my kinsman's drawing?" inquired Guaracco of Lorenzo. "Truly, he has rich and varied talents. Surely he has told you of that other matter he hopes to develop, the science of flying."

"Flying?" repeated Simonetta Vespucci, her magnificent eyes suddenly bright.

"Aye, that," said Guaracco. "With a machine called a plane."

He used the Twentieth-Century English word, and I must have started visibly. It was plain that Guaracco had picked my brains well.

Simonetta laughed incredulously. "Doubtless this young man proposes to soar with wings to those great worlds and suns he pretends to see in the sky."

"Might it not be sacrilege?" Giuliano garnished his lady's apparent effort to confuse me. "Flight is contrary to man's nature."

Guaracco's smile derided me too, and I felt a touch of anger. "How contrary?" I demanded of Giuliano. "Is it more contrary than to ride comfortably and swiftly on the back of a horse?"

Abbot Mariotto came to my support. "The young man has reason on his side," he spoke up, between sips of wine. "Holy Writ says of the righteous: 'They shall mount up with wings as eagles', and, in another place: 'O, that I had wings like a dove!' Surely flight would not be ungodly, if it were not done by black magic."

"Well, Ser Leo?" Lorenzo prompted me, leaning back in his great cushioned chair with one long knobby leg crossed over the other.

"Magnificence, there is no such thing as black magic," I pronounced, "neither in my devices nor elsewhere."

Every eye widened, and Guaracco twitched angrily, as though I had pricked him with a needle. But I had determined to make amends to my own self-respect, because of my earlier, unwilling words in his praise, and because he had succeeded in frightening me.

"Of all human discourses," I elaborated warmly, speaking to Lorenzo but gazing with a defiant eye at Guaracco, "the most foolish is that which affirms a belief in necromancy." I refused to let Guaracco silence me with a hostile glare. "If black magic truly existed," I went on, "he who controlled it would be lord of all nations. No human skill could resist him. Buried treasures and the jewels of Earth's heart would lie revealed to him. No lock, no fortress, could remain shut against his will. He could travel the uttermost parts of the Universe." I spread my hands triumphantly. "But why go on, adding instance to instance? What could not be brought to pass by such a magician, if the foolish tales of magic were true?"

There were smiles among the ladies and mutters

among the men; but Lorenzo smote his palms together in applause. "Handsomely said," he pronounced, like a judge rendering a decision. "Do you
not agree, Guaracco? Does this not prove that there
are no sorcerers?"

"It proves, at least, my own innocence of sorcery."
Guaracco bowed, to give his words graceful emphasis.
"If I could do such things, would I be so humble and
loyal and dependent a servant of Your Magnificence?
Surely," and his eyes stared back into mine, "nothing
would be impossible to a true necromancer."

"Nothing," I agreed bleakly, meeting his gaze,
"except refuge from death."

Guaracco's smile vanished, like a light blown out.

Lorenzo nibbled a sweetmeat. "This bethinks me,
friends. One matter has not yet been understood. Ser
Leo is scarce more than a boy, a student of the arts
and a wondrously eloquent authority on the sciences.
Yet he conquered with ease my nonpareil swordsman,
poor Gido. That comes close to tasting of enchant-
ment."

Again I spread my hands, in one of the free Florentine gestures I was beginning to adopt. "I say again,
Magnificence, that it was naught but skill."

"We must make trial." Lorenzo permitted himself
a grin.

I must have looked somewhat worried, for Giuliano burst out into confident laughter and stepped
forward, hand on the jeweled hilt of his sword. "Suf-

fer me to do the trying," he said, his gay, handsome face eager in the white glare of the lamps.

Simonetta's silvery laugh greeted this challenge by her cavalier. The abbot also called out for this unchurchmanly demonstration to go forward at once. Before I knew what was happening, the chairs, benches and other furniture had been thrust back to clear a space. The ladies stood together, each holding up a lamp to give better light. I found myself facing the merry-eyed, confident Giuliano. Poliziano had hurried off to fetch something, and now he returned and thrust a hard object into my right fist.

"Show us how you defend yourself, young sir," he bade me.

Giuliano drew his sword and wadded his embroidered cloak into a protection upon his free arm. I transferred my own weapon to my left hand. As I did so, I saw that it was a mere cane of hard wood, of a sword's length—such a cudgel as I had watched young Florentine apprentices use in their hit-or-miss fencing exercises. Giuliano, on the other hand, had unsheathed a blade that was one of the finest and sharpest I had ever seen. Plainly, I was to furnish sport for this gallant and his friends, with all the advantages on his side..

Because I must, I lifted my wooden stick to the salute, then slanted it to cross his steel. Lorenzo hummed in his throat. "Your cousin is sinister-handed,

Guaracco," he observed. "That may be the secret of his skill."

"I count him no danger for that," said Giuliano, with unmalicious zest, then disengaged and thrust at me.

Quite plainly he meant business. The keen point would have nicked and wounded my breast had I not shortened my own guard to deflect it. Cheers went up from the ladies, then turned into dismayed cries, as, extending my parry to its swift conclusion as a riposte, I smote Giuliano smartly on the inside of the right elbow.

He wheezed and sprang back out of reach. Had I followed instantly and struck again, I might have forced him to drop his sword. But I reminded myself that I had to do with the second greatest man in Florence; lest I anger him, I contented myself with standing on guard.

Again Giuliano laughed. "God's faith, what a tingler! But you'll have hard work to do it another time, Ser Leo."

He advanced again, very much the practiced fencer, his cloaked arm brought well up. I waited as before until his thrust came, parried it and drove it out of line, and again sped my riposte. He interposed the folds of his cloak, taking a muffled tap on his left forearm, and retreated. This time I followed him, avoided an engagement and half struck at his head.

But then I checked myself, lest I injure him and make dangerous enemies among those who watched. Instead, I diverted my stroke into a sweeping moulinet, passing over his point to my right, and got home with a resounding whack on Giuliano's velvet-sleeved sword arm.

Absolute silence fell, then a babble of consternation from the onlookers; for Giuliano's smile had vanished, and with it his good will for me.

Plainly the contest had ceased abruptly to be sport with him. Stung and ruffled by my thumps, he uttered a soft blasphemy. Then he advanced quickly and sped a slashing cut —not at me, but at my stick. The edge of his sword, sharp as a whetstone could make it, shore through the tough wood as through a parsnip, and I was left with a mere truncated billet, no more than fifteen inches long, in my hand.

"No, no, Giuliano!" shouted Lorenzo in protest, but too late to balk his brother's vicious stab at my throat.

I managed to parry with the short stub of wood remaining to me, causing his point to shoot upward and over my left shoulder. In the same instant, I stepped quickly in, almost against him as he extended his body in the lunge. Before he could recover, my right hand caught the cross guard of his weapon, and I wrenched with all my strength. His own right arm, bruised twice already, had been weakened. I tore the sword from his grasp.

At once I dropped the bit of stick and whipped the captured hilt into my left hand.

"Borrow a blade from one of your friends, my lord Giuliano," I panted fiercely, "and, by your leave, we will continue on something like terms of fairness."

But then Lorenzo, Poliziano and Guaracco had sprung forward to pull us away from each other. The sorcerer's big hands were at my shoulders hustling me back, his red beard rasped my ear as he hissed a warning to take care. Lorenzo the Magnificent was lecturing Giuliano in the fashion of older brothers to younger, in every land and generation. And Giuliano recovered his lost temper.

"Hark you," he called out to me, "I did amiss. I had no lust to hurt you at the beginning, I meant only fun. And then —" He broke off, smiling and nodding, and rubbing his bruised arm. "Then it was fun no longer, and I forgot myself," he confessed frankly. "Not many there are who can teach me either weapon-play or good manners, but, by Saint Michael of the Sword! You have taught me both, and I stand your debtor."

With that, he brushed Guaracco aside and embraced me in the impulsive Latin manner. I thanked him and offered him his sword again, but he shook his handsome dark head. "Nay, keep it as a token of fellowship between us," he insisted. He unbuckled his jeweled belt with the dangling sheath, and strapped it about my own waist. "Hear me, all! From this moment, Leo and I are friends."

The company sank into chairs again, happy that no harm had befallen either of us.

"We wander from our earlier discourses," reminded Abbot Mariotto, with what he may have thought to be tact. "You spoke, my son Leo, of a machine that could fly. Where is it?"

"It is not constructed, Holy Father," I replied. "I do but have hopes."

For, as with so many other things, the principle of flying a heavier-than-air machine was caught only vaguely at the jumbled back of my head. I could visualize the form but roughly—a thin body with a rudder for tail and outspread wings; and there would be something to stir the air and pull the machine forward. Beyond that I could think of nothing, for design or power.

"You would strap wings to your arms?" suggested Giuliano.

"No, no," objected Poliziano. "Are not men's arms too weak for flight? Would they not need great muscles, at least as strong as those of the legs?"

"Nay, do not speak to me of the weakness of Leo's arms," Giuliano said, with a wry laugh. "I find that they are strong enough to serve his purpose, at fighting or flying."

I had an inspiration of sorts, and I hoped it might answer. "The muscles of our legs are many times

stronger than needful for the support of the weight
of our bodies," I began.

Lorenzo, eager as always for new philosophic diversion, challenged me to prove it on the spot. I asked
for a long plank of wood, and while servants went
scurrying to fetch it, I chose a strong, straight chair
and sat upon it. I took a cushion and laid it upon my
knees, planting my feet firmly. When the plank arrived, I balanced it upon the cushion.

"Now come, all of you," I invited, "and seat your-
selves upon this plank."

Lorenzo did so at once, and then Giuliano. The
others followed, laughing at the sport—not excepting
Madonna Simonetta and the holy abbot—until ten
weights in all were supported upon my knees. Only
Guaracco stood aloof.

"Those long shanks of yours support many hun-
dredweight, and that of the greatest and most tal-
ented humanity in Tuscany," he said, "but what does
this prove, my stalwart cousin?"

"It proves Leo's argument, and the fallacy of
mine," replied Poliziano for me, as he rose from his
seat at one end of the plank; the others followed suit
gracefully, letting none spill. "His legs may have ten-
fold strength, and his arms, by that same token, may
well be strong in proportion, enough to fly upward
with his entire weight supported upon wings."

"Then let me see it done," commanded Lorenzo,
with a finality that made my heart sink. "I am ambi-

tious, Ser Leo, to watch you mount up with wings
as eagles. Nor do I forget that other arrangement you
promised me, the shot that will explode among
enemy soldiers."

This latter problem, which earlier I had been glad
to slight in conversation, now actually seemed the
easier to perform.

But Simonetta and the lady in green professed
themselves weary of so much cold science, be it ever
so important in a masculine world, and begged for
music. Poliziano took up a silver-clasped lute, picked
out a lively tune, and sang in a voice as sweet as his
appearance was ungainly. His song was saucy and
merry, and not a little shocking; but Abbot Mariotto
himself led the laughter.

"More, I pray you!" cried Simonetta.

Poliziano bowed to her, and sang, to a more measured and melodious tune, a set of verses that plainly
were impromptu. They mentioned the beauty of
Simonetta, the benign rule of Lorenzo, the dignity
and piety of Abbot Mariotto, and, finally, the enigmatic fascination of my own discourse.

"And will not Ser Leo sing next?" asked the lady
in green when Poliziano had finished. "His conversation and talents are so varied —war, science, debate,
flying like a bird."

"Aye, young sir, let us hear your voice," Lorenzo
urged me.

Thus invited, I took Poliziano's lute, altering the

pitch and harmony of its four strings until I could strum upon it in a simple fashion to evoke chords for my own accompaniment. The song, which I managed to devise on the spot and sing to Poliziano's tune, was on the subject of stars, so edifying to my new friends and so distasteful to Guaracco. Since Lorenzo and the others commended it highly, it may not be amiss to set it down here:

You think I am a spark—I am a star.
You think that I am small—but I am great.
You think me dim—but I am only far,
Far out in space, beyond your love or hate.

You think me feeble—but I am a sun
Whose rule is resolute, whose face endures,
Beneath whose heat and light are wonders done
Throughout a leash of nobler worlds than yours.

You think you know my secrets, and you say
That they are thus and thus—but, through the sky,
My beam strikes from so many years away,
You know not how I live, nor when I die.

X. THE BOMBS AND THE WINGS

As we departed together from Lorenzo's garden, Guaracco spoke with grim irony:

"It comes to my mind that I know something, after all, of how you live," he said, "and that it is not beyond me to arrange when and how you die."

"Your threats are so frequent that they become wearisome," I rejoined, for my fear of him had quite departed. "In any case, your masterful ways displease me, and I will have no more of them." And I stopped on the mossy path, my hand seeking the hilt of the sword Giuliano had given me.

"No violence," he warned quickly. "You have that handful of steel at your belt, but I carry the short gun you saw yesterday. And my dwarfs are never far away."

"Killing me would be awkward for you," I told him. "You heard Giuliano de' Medici swear that he and I were close friends, and Lorenzo thinks I will be a valuable associate. Never doubt but that they would ask most disturbing questions about any hurt to me."

His beard stirred in the gloom, and I knew that he smiled. "Oh, I do not intend to kill you unless you force me. And all these defiances of yours stand to my profit."

"Your profit?" I echoed, for, after my temporary semi-hypnotized plea to Lorenzo for him, nothing had been further from my mind than to bring profit to Guaracco.

"Aye, that. In speaking scornfully of magic, and upholding natural science, you taught me a lesson—and, as with Giuliano, few can boast of teaching me anything of worth. The time draws near, I think, when I should forget my sorcery-pretense, at least where it concerns my traffic with Lorenzo. Science shall be my way with him hereafter. You and I will work wonders for His Magnificence, the two of us."

"You dare think that I will help you?"

He laughed. "It is I who will help you, Leo. For instance, in that matter of the explosive shot, I saw, as did not Lorenzo, that you were perplexed. But it happens that I may assist you to fashion such a thing, and more wondrous things afterward."

"You have noted down and rationalized my half-lost memories," I accused.

"And you should thank me heartily for doing so. Do you not still wish to return some day to your own century?"

It was useless to deny that, I knew.

"For instance," went on Guaracco, "you have forgotten certain ways to use this strange power you name to me as electricity. It gives light, does it not? How, then?"

I could not tell him, and glumly admitted as much.

"Then suffer me to refresh that lost memory of yours. Is there not a certain bottle, or globe, of glass, exhausted of air, and a wire of some substance set glowing within —"

I clutched his arm, so suddenly fierce that he swore in startled pain. "You learned that from me when you enslaved my mind. Yes, I had forgotten utterly, but you know. And you know, too, about aircraft. You steal my wits from me!"

"Hands off," he growled back. "Do not seem to quarrel with me. Here come Lorenzo's grooms with our horses."

We mounted and rode away side by side.

"You will call to mind that I showed you a pearl," resumed Guaracco as we entered a dim street, lighted only by the lanterns of a watch patrol. "It was a beautiful jewel, you thought. And it gave you the most restful of slumber."

That confirmed my earlier judgment of his methods, and again I braced my inner defenses lest he try another occult conquest of my mind and spirit. But he only nodded as he rode, as though to check the point.

"I learned things about your science which you yourself seem unable to grasp when awake. Leo, you will look into that pearl again."

"Never," I said stonily.

"Oh, do not be an utter fool. We could produce marvels for Lorenzo, and win great favor and great wealth. And at last, we could build your time reflector. Nay," he corrected himself, "call it *our* time reflector. It is the only way we can do it, by use of the pearl. Then we can contrive to journey together, forward through the ages, and I shall be your guest in your century, as you have been my guest in mine."

There was some sense in his argument, and I found most pleasant the thought of what I might do to him, once I had him in the year 1957 and with the advantages on my side. But still I resented his absorbing mastery of every situation between us. As on other occasions, he seemed to read my mind.

"Come, Leo, let us not be master and servant any longer," he pleaded, "but colleagues and friends. Lorenzo is disposed to grant money for a workshop of our own. Meanwhile, you can stay on with Verrocchio, lest others become suspicious of our mysteries. But your spare time can apply to both our profits." His voice became crafty. "Lisa asked after you today. And, for all your harsh words to her, I dare think you would be pleased to see her again. Is this not so?"

Of course it was so. But I could not think romantically of her while I thought of escaping from the Renaissance. Finally, I agreed to a truce and a partnership. Guaracco talked on eagerly, offering me concessions and assurances.

On the following day, I skimped my work with Verrocchio and called at the little house where Guaracco had tried to bestow Lisa upon me. It was Lisa who met me at the door, and as she recognized me, she showed her shy smile, but the smile was happy and hopeful.

How, I asked myself, had I been able to admire Simonetta Vespucci so greatly? Here, in Lisa, was a greater beauty, a beauty that glowed without scorching, that was powerful without ostentation. Almost I said as much to her as I stood on the threshold. Then I thought again that Guaracco must not be given a chance to use Lisa as a weapon against me.

"Happy am I to see you again, Madonna," I contented myself with telling her.

"Come in, my dear cousin, come in," called Guaracco heartily from behind her. "I have been waiting here for you to come and help."

As at his house in the country, Guaracco had fitted up the cellar of his city dwelling as a laboratory and machine shop. We began at once to work on the explosive shot which Lorenzo had commissioned.

At my recommendation, we made the case cylindrical instead of round, eighteen inches long and six in diameter. Bronze, being light, strong and workable, was our choice for this part of the work. When we had cut and shaped and brazed it, I chiseled deep cross lines in the outer surface so that it might fly the more readily into pieces when the inner charge exploded. This case we filled with lumps of lead, with spaces between for powder.

Guaracco, though helpful, was as puzzled as Giuli-

ano de' Medici concerning the delay in the explosion.
To make certain of that delay, I mixed a slow-burning powder, using charcoal of willow wood only
lightly burnt. The completed mixture was no more
than dark brown in color, and our experiments
proved that a noticeable interval of time was needed
for its ignition. Of this slow-burning powder I made
a fuse or match, wrapped in silk, which led through
a hole at the rear part of the bomb casing.

"The discharge of the powder in the cannon will
ignite the match," I explained, "and the shot itself
will explode in as short a time as you would need to
say an Ave Maria."

"Say an Ave Maria for the souls of those it strikes."

When we had finished the bomb, we made another,
more elaborate. Its curved sides were pierced with
muzzles, through which bullets could be thrown by
the explosion. When both of these were finished—
their manufacture occupied only a morning and an
afternoon—Guaracco recommended that we wait
before presenting them to Lorenzo the Magnificent.

"I take a parable from the construction itself," he
said to me. "Let us delay the explosion of this cunning device, and it will be the more effective with
His Magnificence. Remember, too, that when you
have given him the explosive shot, he will demand
all the more insistently that you build the flying
machine."

That was excellent advice. I was still muddled in

my notion of man-lifting wings, and Guaracco could not—or would not—help me.

Therefore, I went into the trading centers of Florence to shop for materials. My teacher, Andrea del Verrocchio, who had heard little and understood less of my problem, nevertheless made the good suggestion that I use as framework the wood of Spanish yew. It was employed, as he reminded me, by the archers of England for their superb longbows, and was undoubtedly the strongest wood for its weight to be had. I purchased a bundle of yew staves, which I shaped and thinned by careful whittling, and chose light, strong silk for the fabric.

My best model, it seemed to me, would be the wing of a bat. I went so far as to snare and kill several bats —sorrowfully, for I love animals —and by manipulating their wings and bodies, I found out certain principles of flight. These I demonstrated by small-scale models, to be hung on threads and made to simulate wing-action by a strong blast of air from a bellows. A new problem added itself to that of the wings, the construction and operation of the tail as a rudder. I sketched out a design like a fan, which I proposed to control by the motion of pressure of the feet.

Guaracco professed a great deal of interest in this work of mine, which took up all my spare time for days. His interest seemed to partake of superior amusement, as though he foresaw ludicrous failure. Lisa, on the other hand, admired and encouraged.

"Can I help you in any way?" she asked me.

"Aye, that," I replied thankfully. "In the first hour of our meeting, you showed yourself skillful with the needle. Perhaps you can help sew my fabric for me."

"Happy am I if I can do so," she said, gravely sweet.

I joined the ribs of the wings and tail, with looped pieces of leather at the main junctures and lesser bindings of raw silk. Lisa fitted, cut and sewed the silk to perfection. It was a delight to see her at work.

It was late in the summer of 1470 —the latter part of August, as I recollect —that I tried my mechanism.

For greater privacy, we returned to Guaracco's country house, the scene of my first appearance after my reflection through time. Guaracco led the way on his splendid white stallion. I rode the gray that had belonged to my hapless adversary Gido. Lisa had a pretty little mule, and grooms with other mules managed the unwieldy bundles that held my wings and rudder.

How and when Guaracco's two dwarfs made the journey, I do not know. I had thought that we left them behind in Florence, but they were waiting for us when we dismounted at the country house.

After a light noon meal of cold meat, bread and white wine, I went to a tall shed at the rear of the house. Scrambling up, I donned my pinions. From tip to tip they measured full forty feet, and I fastened them to me with strong, light straps under the armpits, around my biceps and to my wrists. There were springy grips for my hands to clutch, and by relaxing or applying squeeze-pressure, I could spread or fold, like an umbrella, the ribs that supported the fabric. The tail I fixed to my legs, with stirrup-like clasps around my insteps. I could straddle to extend the fan, or bring my feet together to collapse it.

I gazed down at the ground. It seemed a long way off just then. Beneath me stood Lisa, her lovely oval face full of apprehension; and at an upper window of the house, Guaracco thrust out his red beard to watch.

"Ready," I said to myself. "Now."

I sprang. As I did so, I spread and beat the wings, extended the tail downward and outward to give me direction in my soaring. There was a sickening, airy moment in space. My eyes turned upward to the sun. I seemed to feel the world grow small beneath me. Another and longer moment, with the touch of triumph, another frantic beating thrash of the wings.

Then I whirled helplessly, and fell.

I suppose I was stunned. There was a galvanizing shock and darkness to swallow me, and, from far away, laughter, the delighted laughter of Guaracco. Then another voice, soft and gentle and tremulous. Lisa was pattering a prayer to the saints.

Struggling with my close-clamped eyelids, I managed to see again. I lay pillowed upon sweet softness, and Lisa's face bent close above mine, all white except for the worried blue eyes, the quivering lips. She had taken my drumming head into her lap, and her fingers touched my brow. "Thank the high heavens you are not dead!" she sobbed.

"Nay, not I," I assured her, and sat up. That was difficult, for I was bruised in all my limbs, and those laboriously fashioned wings were shattered and broken.

Guaracco descended from his post at the window, and strolled out into the yard, grinning. "By my faith, Leo, not Icarus himself plunged so tragically from the sky."

I managed to regain my feet, and bent to unstrap the tangle of wreckage. "Yet, for a moment, I flew," I vowed. "The next time —"

"Must there be a next time?" interrupted Lisa, trembling again. "I pray the saints that you do not seek to fly again."

"Ah, how prettily she pleads," observed Guaracco, stroking his beard. "Leo, are you not content to remain upon the ground and near her? Will you not leave flight to the birds, its proper masters?"

But I shook my head stubbornly, making it ache more painfully. "Not I," I told them both. "A bird is no more than an instrument that works by mathematical law. It is within the capacity of man's mind to duplicate that instrument, and the working of it. I shall try again, and I shall succeed."

"May it be my good fortune to watch the sport of your next trial," snickered Guaracco.

But he was more helpful when, in the house, I stripped off my doublet and revealed bruised ribs and shoulders. His many skills included the mixing of salves and ointments, and the sticky stuff he applied to my hurts gave them immediate relief.

"We have the bombs, at least, to offer to Lorenzo," he reminded me.

XI. HOPES OF ESCAPE

Bombs, of a primitive sort, were known to armorers of Florence, but Lorenzo was highly pleased when he received ours. He gave us an audience, and later he entertained us on the terrace of his splendid villa in the pleasant green suburb of Fiesole.

"These engines would do us credit in any battle," he was gracious enough to say. "Yet it is my hope to see some more peaceable invention of yours, Leo. What, for example, of that flying machine?"

"I make slow progress." I attempted to put him off, and Guaracco also labored to change the subject. We discussed the summer heat, and the threatened drying up of wells in Florence.

"If it please Your Magnificence," I made bold to suggest, "an irrigation plan might be drawn up. The waters of the Arno could supply the town in the driest season, and water the fields as well."

"If such a plan were successful, it would greatly ease the trouble of my beautiful Florence," said Lorenzo, and again I thought how his smile softened the arresting ugliness of his face.

"Again," I pursued, "does it not seem well to widen the streets of the town? A street should be no less wide than the houses are high."

"Make haste slowly," he bade me. "Finish the flying machine before you turn Florence into a paradise for angels."

But an early autumn, with real Tuscany frost, enabled me to ask for time and brighter, warmer weather. As winter came on, I lived in Florence, and under Verrocchio I worked at paintings, statues, metal work and wood carving. In the evenings I found plenty of diversion, for Sandro Botticelli and Giuliano de' Medici both showed themselves ready to sponsor me in the society of noble families.

I was often entertained at great mansions. Several times Lorenzo summoned me to his palace for informal dinner and hours of discussion, and once I was invited to the house of Simonetta Vespucci herself.

True, on that occasion she gave most of her time and attention to Giuliano, and I saw nothing of her husband, who was either complaisant or utterly dim-witted; but Botticelli introduced me to Simonetta's kinsman by marriage, Amerigo Vespucci. He was no older than I, a great parader of his education by Dominican friars, and he had begun to win fame as a geographer and map maker. He had brought as a guest a tall, roan-haired young man from Genoa, a sailor and adventurer.

"Messer Cristoforo Colombo," Vespucci introduced him to Botticelli and me, as we stood warming ourselves before an open fire of aromatic wood.

"Colombo?" I repeated. The name did things to my distorted recollections. "Colombo? Hark you, sir, you intend to follow the sea all your days?"

"Aye, that." The roan-haired Genoese nodded, smiling. "It is the life I love most, and I have sailed far. I have visited the infidel princes to the east, and I have been to Spain and France, even to England. I hope to go to more distant lands some day."

"More distant lands?" I exclaimed eagerly. "Aye, and that you shall do —go to more distant lands." In my earnestness, I laid a hand on his broad shoulder. "Messer Cristoforo," I said, "much of the world but waits, unclaimed, undreamed of, until you search and find it."

"Indeed?" he said, mystified.

"There are whole continents besides these we know of," I plunged ahead, "whole oceans and shoals of islands. It is fated for you to sail westward, to find a new world!"

"How, a new world?" asked Botticelli.

"This Earth of ours is round," I informed the three of them weightily. "It is shaped like a ball, with oceans and lands at every quarter of it. In circumference it is nearly twenty-five thousand miles."

Colombo burst into laughter at that, so heartily that Botticelli and Amerigo Vespucci both stared at him.

"I have it now, Messer Leo," said Colombo. "You

have been reading that strange book by the Englishman."

"What strange book, sir?" I demanded, puzzled in
my turn.

"John Mandeville was the Englishman's name, and
he wrote his tale of wondrous travels a good hundred
years ago. Now, I bethink me, he even said the circumference of the round Earth is something near
your measurement, more than twenty thousand English miles. But to my mind, it is smaller than that,
with India's most eastern spice islands not too many
days' sailing out from the Azores."

"You tell us nothing new, young sir," Vespucci
said to me. "Surely only the simple countryfolk, and
empty-headed court sparks with no wit to see truth,
cling to the ancient belief that the Earth is flat. The
journey of the sun and stars, the dropping down of
a vessel's hull at the line of sky and sea, these prove
the roundness of the Earth."

"And so might I have proved by a voyage, had
some prince but given me ships," added Colombo
wistfully.

"I can assure you of your ships," I felt forced to
say. "In the year 1492 —"

"By your leave, my friend," he said, with a bow,
"I shall wait for that happy day to dawn before I feel
certain of it."

And that incident went far toward curing me of
the making of prophecies.

To satisfy Lorenzo, I continued to fashion new devices that might appease him when he complained that I was long at work on my flying machine. The most popular, to peasants and porters, as well as to my companions on a higher social scale, was the wheelbarrow.

As to my studies in the arts, I was able to contribute many suggestions which Verrocchio accepted gratefully. Among them was the rather obvious one that a painter or sculptor of the living figure should study anatomy. Such investigation was extremely difficult in Florence, for religious law frowned upon the cutting up of bodies that should have Christian burial.

However, once again Lorenzo was ready to assist me, and gave me permission to visit morgues, to study and even to dissect bodies of paupers. Some of my anatomical sketches Verrocchio posted on the walls of his *bottega* for the instruction of other students, and we also assembled upon a pedestal the complete skeleton of a horse, to aid in making equestrian figures.

When the spring of 1471 followed the winter, Lorenzo entertained Galeazzo Maria Sforza, Duke of Milan, in lavish manner. Andrea del Verrocchio was pageant master during those glittering days, and I was one of his chief assistants in planning processions of horsemen and elaborately costumed figures, routs,

balls, receptions and miracle plays, and even a warlike afternoon of jousting in one of the public
squares.

Here, banks of seats were erected all around a clear
space, so that the square represented a stadium or
hippodrome; and various Florentine cavaliers tilted
against the followers of the Milanese tyrant. Lorenzo
offered, in what he must have thought a kindly mood,
to provide me with armor, a lance and a war horse,
so that I might take part in the trial of arms. When
I declined, he thought that I was being modest.

"You are an artist and a scientist, and my friend,"
he argued, "and therefore, among free Florentines at
least, the peer of any gentleman in Duke Galeazzo's
train. Do not be humble before these lords and their
lances."

But I managed to beg off, though the spot was not
so dangerous as I had expected. For one thing, the
opposing cavaliers did not gallop full upon each
other. They rode along opposite sides of a paling,
endeavoring to strike or push across it with land
point against shield or helmet.

For another thing, professional soldiers were
barred, as apt to forget themselves and cause regret-
table accidents. The dashing and handsome Giuliano
de' Medici headed the Florentine contingent. He
wore a knot of gay ribbon, tied upon his mailed arm
by the beautiful Simonetta Vespucci, and he over-

threw two opponents. All in all, the jousting struck me as rather tame.

Lorenzo, too, was no more than hospitable in his attendance at these exercises; he took a more special pride in showing his art treasures to the visiting duke, who, as Poliziano later told me, cried out that mere gold and silver could not approximate such treasures of the soul. When at length the Milanese departed, they were too greatly impressed to hide their admiration, which was precisely what pleased Lorenzo.

Guaracco had insinuated himself into many of the revels. It had been his earnest hope to make a friend of Galeazzo Sforza, but after a carefully contrived interview on the final day of the visit, he sought me out at Verrocchio's *bottega*, shaking his head.

"Yonder Sforza tyrant is too absolute a master among his Milanese," he complained. "He offered me only money."

"Is money not something?" I rallied him, for in those days he and I were on terms of something that resembled good fellowship.

Again he shook his red head. "Money is little, in itself. I want power."

"So I have heard you say, Guaracco."

"I want wills to be bowed to mine," he plunged on. "Cities to rise or fall at my lifted hand, great men to go on errands here and there in the world with my commands on their lips. I want the ocean to shake with the passage of my fleets; the continents to vibrate under the marching of my armies. I want to rule!"

"But money rules," I reminded him. "Look at Lorenzo. The founder of his house was a druggist, a simple maker of pills. Yet, by the accumulation and wise use of gold —"

"Gold!" snorted Guaracco. "It buys food, clothes, wine, music, flattery —but what value is it beyond those things? It was powerful with the Medici only through generations of careful planning. I cannot wait so long. Cold steel is the better metal, if held by a brave man and ruled by a wise one."

This was more than I had ever heard before of the inner ambition of this charlatan-genius.

"I followed sorcery from boyhood," he went on, "because, at first, I believed in it. As you yourself once said, a true sorcerer could travel the winds, chain the lightnings, know and rule all men. Even when I grew wiser, I still studied the black art."

"Well?"

"You know my coven of witch-worshippers. They serve me in many ways—through fear, or awe, or fascination—that they would not dare dream of if I offered them only gold. Many nobles and merchants respect and fear me because I seem to foretell events, cast horoscopes, and apparently summon devils. One or two are well within my power."

"But now you say you follow true science, and see sorcery as false."

"*Is* there no such thing as real sorcery, Leo? Come with me."

Again I accompanied him to his house nearby. The front room was changed; there was a massive square table with a thick velvet covering extending to the floor on all sides. In its center stood a great bowl of silver-coated glass.

Guaracco drew the heavy curtains at the windows, so that the room was quite dark, and scraped flint and steel to light a candle. Then, at the clap of his hands, the two dwarfs entered with a great ewer of water between them. From this, Guaracco filled the bowl to the brim.

"Look into it, Leo," he bade me as the dwarfs departed, and I did so.

"How then?" I challenged him. "Here is a simple basin of water."

"You are sure? Thrust in your hands and convince yourself."

Again I obeyed him. It was water, sure enough, and beneath it the surface of the bowl was smooth and hard. "I see no wonder."

"What did you expect to find in that bowl? The face of Lisa?" And he laughed. "Favor me, kinsman, by blowing out the candle."

I blew it out. The room fell all dark at once. No,

not all, for a faint filtered glow rose from the bowl of water.

"A chemical trick," I pronounced. "You have put phosphorus in there."

"Did you not see the water poured from the ewer? But I make no argument. Look into the bowl again."

As he spoke, he put his own great hand into the water and stirred it into ripples. Gazing, I saw nothing but a disturbed surface, like a tiny ocean in a gale, with light beneath. Then the ripples grew less and departed. I gazed deep into the radiant water.

From its bottom a face looked up at me.

Lisa . . .

I spoke her name aloud, and put forth a hand to touch her forehead. But my fingers dipped only into water, and Guaracco laughed his familiar mocking peal.

"Ha, you were deceived, for all your assurance," he taunted me. Quickly he moved to uncurtain the windows, brightening the room. "See how simply it was arranged? I did it an hour ago, to mystify and impress one of the Milanese nobles. A hole in the table, a glass bottom in the bowl, and, under the velvet, a couch whereon Lisa lay with a light beside her —"

He lifted the table cover, and Lisa crept out.

"You looked upon her as through a window," summed up Guaracco, and then laughed again. "Nay,

Leo, she did not deceive you of her own thought. I put her to sleep, as you know I can do, with this."

He held it up in his fingers, the glowing pearl that more than once had drawn forth my wits. Staring at it unguardedly, I felt myself ensnared before I could resist. Guaracco caught my elbow and eased me into a chair as mists closed about me.

When I awoke, Guaracco sat at the velvet-covered table, scribbling hastily upon sheets of white paper.

"You will rejoice," he said, seeing my eyes open. "I took opportunity to explore again that closed memory of yours."

"What, this time?"

"Details of your time reflector."

At once I lost my resentment of his sly assertion of power over my senses. "Full details?"

"Enough, I think, to build the machine itself."

And then I saw Lisa's eyes turned mournfully upon me, as though already she bade me farewell.

XII. THE NEW REFLECTOR

Even if I could, I do not think I would set down exact specifications for a machine which is so apt to cause trouble as the one for which Guaracco gleaned the theory from the waste places of my mind. The fact is, he kept the plans to himself, and questioned me only now and then. Sometimes he hypnotized me for the questioning, sometimes not. And there were problems which even he could not comprehend.

"These exact measurements for the parts of the steel frame, how can we achieve them?" he would ask. "You tell, in your sleep, of micrometers; yet how can we design a micrometer? How, even knowing its principle, can we make it without proper tools? How was the first micrometer made?"

Automatic lathes, alloy charts and welding torches were similarly unattainable. Guaracco did the next best thing. He sought out a master swordsmith, and in some adroit way —I think his witch-cult helped him —bound the man to his service by terror and awe. This craftsman, with all his tools and materials, Guaracco transported to our country workshop, and there set him to the painstaking task of shaping the metal skeleton of the reflector mechanism.

Electrical engineering, Guaracco was obliged to learn from the ground up; I must needs be hypnotized again and again, and my subconscious mind probed for what it could furnish. Guaracco began with sticks of sealing wax and glass rods, rubbing them with fur and silk, and studying the effects of the static charges. From that, he progressed to what I was able to remember as a Leyden jar, contrived by his own cunning hands after repeated unsuccessful trials. Finally came simple batteries, but here he kept back from me the knowledge he had mined from my own inhibited psyche. He refused to tell the acids and metals involved.

While I wrangled over his stubborn secrecy, a messenger from Lorenzo appeared, to ask how I progressed with the flying machine.

"You reminded him of that," I accused Guaracco in private.

"Faith, Leo, how ungrateful you are." He grinned unabashedly, hand to his red beard. "Go to Florence and make your report to His Magnificence. I will work here in our laboratory, and I promise you that when you return I will have heartening progress to show."

To Florence, perforce, I went. Lorenzo received me with some impatience, in his frescoed audience-chamber at the palace.

"Well, young sir, and what of the wings you are

to make?" he demanded. "I gave you and Guaracco money for your experiments, and it is high time that you tendered me some return."

I exhibited my small models, all I had to show since the breaking of my first wings. He was interested but not satisfied, and once again I bitterly regretted having mentioned aviation to this ambitious and imaginative tyrant. Yet, as I knew, men could make themselves able to fly. I had seen them, in that age whence I had come and which itself was yet to dawn —men flying singly or in parties, with the aid of great spread-pinioned contrivances.

Meanwhile, Lorenzo was issuing orders. "I shall see this device take shape under my own eyes. At my villa in Fiesole is a great guest house. Go you thither, Ser Leo, set up your shop, and have sent to you all that you need. Work where I can come and watch."

I bowed acceptance, and went to Fiesole. There, messengers brought me the broken remains of my wings and rudder, also more leather, staves and silk. Lisa, too, came at my urgent plea, to help, as before, with the sewing.

She made a considerable impression on the various guests who thronged Lorenzo's hospitable villa. Botticelli wanted to paint her, Poliziano celebrated her in verses. Giuliano spoke so courtly to her that Simonetta Vespucci's eyes took on a green glow. And to a certain captain of mercenaries, a Spaniard named

Hernando Villareal who had sought Lorenzo to ask for employment, I was forced to voice a warning.

"The young lady is working on my machine," I told Villareal, "at my wish, and under my protection. She does not welcome your pressing attentions."

"By God's blood," said the Spaniard, and turned to face me under the poplars where we walked aside. "I think, Messer Leo, that it is you who find the situation unpleasant."

"I do not like it, either, if that will content you."

"It does not content me a whit," he said, caressing his long black mustache. "I shall say to Madonna Lisa what I please, whenever I please."

"Few words are best between you and me," I replied. "If you speak to her again, I shall deprive your company of its captain."

And I turned my back on him and walked away.

In a towering rage, he sought for a friend to bear me a formal defiance. The first one he met was Giuliano de' Medici, who had forgotten neither the cudgeling I had given him nor the friendship he had sworn. Giuliano informed the captain that I was the most dangerous antagonist in Christendom, in whose hand a wooden wand was worse than a sword, and a sword itself a pointing finger of Fate. Whereat Captain Hernando Villareal departed Fiesole the same day—indeed, departed Tuscany, and I never heard of him again.

When my wings were completely repaired, and improved in some points, I made a second attempt, springing from the eaves of the guest house while Lorenzo and his friends watched. Again I failed badly, tumbling aslant through the air, but this time I managed to land upright on my feet, only spraining my ankle. My wings and other harness were only slightly damaged, and Guaracco was not present with his ironic laughter.

"I count myself lucky," I said, as Giuliano ran out to support my limping steps. "My ankle will mend of itself. Had my wings broken, they would take more labor and time to be repaired."

"But you have not a complete loss of your attempt," Lorenzo was considerate enough to say. "You came to ground a good ten paces beyond the house—farther, I think, than you might have leaped unaided."

"And had you leaped without wings, you would have had worse hurt than this to your ankle," added Giuliano, forgetting that once he had disputed my theory of man's ability to fly. "For those two moments you were above ground, methought I saw your fabric hold you aloft. At the very least, it broke your fall."

Lisa had hurried to meet me as the two brothers Medici helped me toward the door. Her expression mingled worry over my hurt and relief that I was in no worse plight. I sat on the porch and a physician plucked the shoe from my injured foot.

"I shall yet succeed," I made bold to prophesy. "It is not the fault of my theory, nor yet the weakness of my arms."

"You will learn as a fledgling bird learns," suggested Giuliano.

But my sprained ankle kept me for days at Fiesole, where I could follow no art or science save lute playing and repartee among the silken courtiers. Lisa insisted on remaining with me, most prettily concerned as she bathed and bandaged my injured leg. After a day or so, Guaracco appeared with some of his healing salves, to apply them with a great show of cousinly solicitude, to bow and utter compliments to the ladies, to discuss poetry with Poliziano, weapons with Giuliano, science and philosophy and government with Lorenzo.

"Your Magnificence is generous not to hold against my young cousin these early mishaps at his flying," he said to Lorenzo.

"Nay," replied Lorenzo. "Can he learn as a science, in but a few days, the behavior that has been a born instinct of birds since the creation of the world?"

Guaracco agreed, and with more such talk strengthened Lorenzo's determination that I should continue my efforts to make successful wings. I began to feel that Guaracco considered it to his interest that I do

so. He wanted me to stay at Fiesole, out of his way.
Carefully he arranged that I would not relearn too
much of the science I remembered only in a hypnotic
trance.

For the rest of that summer I was able to put off
a third experiment with my wings —not that I did
not want to fly, but that I dreaded failing again before the disappointed eyes of Lorenzo de' Medici. But
as winter came on, I contrived to please my patron
with other offerings. These included a plan for drain-
ing some nearby swamps, which Lorenzo approved
for the future; a brief written outline of a new system of swordplay for the palace guardsmen, which
Lorenzo in good-humored malice caused me to dem-
onstrate upon two very surprised and glum fencing
masters; and a rather vague suggestion about the use
and purpose of antiseptics for the treatment of
wounds, which Lorenzo could not understand.

I made several attempts also at fashioning both a
microscope and a telescope; but I did not understand
the accurate grinding and adjusting of lenses, and
nobody in Florence was skillful enough to help me.
Also, even when I secured from Andrea del Verrocchio's spectacle-maker a pair of indifferent lenses that
would serve, I could not bring them into proper position at opposite ends of a tube.

One thing I remembered well from reading in my
own century was Mark Twain's pleasant novel about
the Connecticut Yankee in King Arthur's Court. I

failed signally to duplicate the exploits of that blithe and hardheaded adventurer. Perhaps the Yankee, being an adroit and intelligent mechanic, knew the principles of all things from the ground up.

But I didn't; my science had been sketchy, and far too derived. I had been interested in art, so that my less loved readings in chemistry, engineering and physics had been shoved too far back in that clouded brain of mine. Without Guaracco's hypnotism, hardly anything of real complex practicality could be evoked. And under the dreamy spell of the pearl, I was unable to hold until wakefulness any of the things brought to my memory.

Poor Andrea del Verrocchio, who had hoped for so much from my painting and drawing, dared to shake his untidy head over these scientific gropings of mine. "His Magnificence will ruin a master painter to make a convenient artificer," he mourned. And it was true that I had little or no opportunity that winter to paint the picture I had once visioned as my footprint in the sands of Renaissance time.

As for the time reflector, on which Guaracco worked with phenomenal energy and understanding, it took form and power as the cold weather passed us by. Among the things we lacked was a piece of alum large enough to make a lens, but the most notable alum mines of our knowledge were not far away —fifty miles to the southwest, at the ancient town of Volterra.

At that time, however, the Volterrans chose to refuse any trade or tribute to Lorenzo. It began to look as though the only alum we could get must be secured by theft or force.

XIII. THE FATE OF VOLTERRA

Here, indeed, was what seemed a full stop to our
hopes for completing the reflector mechanism. I could
think of nowhere to get alum in a large enough por-
tion, save from a mine. True, crystals may be built
or fed to increase in size, but I did not know how;
and the only available mine in that region was at
Volterra.

That presently defiant city was small, but plucky
and proud, with splendid defenses. Into my musing
mind drifted lines of a poem I had heard repeated in
my other existence:

> . . . lordly Volterra
> Where stands the far-famed hold
> Piled high by hands of giants
> For godlike kings of old.

Whether Volterra's ramparts were built by giants
at the behest of gods, I cannot say; but they were
ancient and strong, what I was to see of them, walls
of rough-cut stone that were said to go back to Etrus-
can times. The city thus enclosed stood upon a huge
olive-clad height, from which the sea was visible a
score of miles distant. Near at hand opened the dark

mouths of those alum mines which were so suddenly forbidden to us as Florentines. In fact, the Volterrans unceremoniously ejected certain commissioners who came from Florence to collect a tribute for Lorenzo.

His Magnificence undoubtedly meant what once he had said to me about wishing to avoid war as costly, dangerous and ignoble—but this was too saucy a challenge for even his considerable patience. In the spring of 1472, he called a meeting of the Signoria —the lot-chosen body of citizens who acted as public council to him —for discussion of the problem. It so happened that Guaracco himself, as a resident of Florence by virtue of that house near Verrocchio's *bottega*, was serving a two-month term with this jury-like group of governors, and he was present at the meeting.

I, too, would have liked to attend, but this was not allowed. Lorenzo had called for a secret session, proof of his concern over Volterra's warlike attitude. All I knew was that one of the Signoria, a pungent old conservative by the name of Tomaso Soderino, intended to speak strongly for conciliation and peace. Perhaps Soderino would show us how to restore friendship with the Volterrans, make it possible for us to secure our alum.

While I waited for news, I wished Lisa were in Florence, to comfort and charm me with her talk and presence. But, with Guaracco's permission, she was visiting a friend, the abbess of a convent near Milan.

The meeting lasted all morning and all afternoon, and the sun was setting as Guaracco came to seek me at Verrocchio's. "It is all settled," he informed me triumphantly.

"Settled?" I repeated. "Peace, you mean?"

"Nay, I mean war. We take our needful alum by force of arms."

I frowned. "But Soderino was going to speak —"

"Aye, and so he did," Guaracco said. "He bleated for hours about soft answers to turn away Volterran wrath, but I had an answer ready. I told Lorenzo, apart, that could not make your flying machine without alum, and plenty of it."

"Alum is not for the flying machine," I protested, "but for the time reflector."

He snapped his big fingers at me. "You do not think I know, boy? But we need alum, and what matter under which pretext we get it? Lorenzo is obsessed with the desire to see men fly. My word was the final ounce in the balance to decide him for war."

Thereafter, things moved fast in Florence. Word arrived that the town of Volterra had employed a thousand tough mercenaries to man her ancient walls. Lorenzo immediately gathered four times that number of troops, and as their commander engaged Federigo d'Urbino, one of the most noteworthy mercenary chieftains of the day.

Lorenzo did not deign to take the field himself, and restrained the younger and more fiery Giuliano from volunteering to lead the mounted lancers. But the brothers Medici did ride at the head of the armed procession through the chief streets of Florence on the day d'Urbino marched against Volterra.

To me, that glittering spectacle was somehow ironic. The cavalry was mostly French and Navarrese, the pike-trailing infantry largely Swiss and Swabian. The crossbow companies were from Sicily; the artillery and siege train were Spanish. The whole cosmopolitan host included sprinklings of Scots, Hungarians, Englishmen and infidel Moors. If any element was missing, it was native Florentine.

Yet so did the Italian city-states fight, not with their own blood but with hired professional adventurers. Something may be said for the system. Battles lacked the extreme ferocity of deadly hate, for opposing generals often were old friends and comrades-in-arms. They proved willing to win or lose, so to speak, on points of strategy. At any rate, Florence's shopkeepers and artisans cheered those foreign soldiers as loudly as though their own sons and brothers were off to war.

Guaracco, as leader of the Signoria's war faction, went to the palace for permission to accompany d'Urbino. I was with him as he found Lorenzo, busily writing at his table in the audience chamber.

"Go if you will," the ruler told Guaracco, without raising his eyes from the page. "I trust that this campaign is decisive."

"You mean, we are to destroy Volterra?" prompted Guaracco, like a lawyer coaxing an admission from a witness.

Lorenzo continued to write, and I thought his work looked like a set of verses. "That physician is often most cruel," he half-murmured, "who appears to be most compassionate."

To this moment, I believe that what he said was being fitted into his poem and did not refer to the coming battle; even if I am mistaken, it was a most equivocal answer. But Guaracco bowed as though he had received specific and welcome orders. Then he hurried away.

I did not ask to go with him, for I had no stomach for war. I felt some uneasy guilt, because with d'Urbino's train of siege ordnance went my multiple cannon arrangement for battering down walls; and many of the crossbowmen carried weapons with the lever improvement Guaracco had learned from me and suggested as his own invention.

A day I lingered in the town, which buzzed excitedly about the campaign. A whole night I lay wakeful in my room at Verrocchio's *bottega*. Something indefinable but insistent preyed on my mind, made me woefully nervous. Dawn had barely become bright when I dressed, drew on thigh-boots and leather riding coat, girded myself with the sword Giuliano had given me and went to fetch my gray horse from the stable.

It was as though a voice summoned me to Volterra.

But I could not ride my poor horse to death. I accomplished no more than thirty-five miles the first day, stopping the night at a peasant's hut. In the morning I continued my journey. Barely an hour on the way, I met another horseman galloping in the direction of Florence. He was a half-armored French lancer, with the velvet-edged sleeves of an under officer. He was three-quarters drunk, to boot, and waved a grubby wine bottle at me.

"Way! Way!" he bawled. "I bear messages to Lorenzo the Magnificent of what happened at Volterra!"

I spurred to meet him and caught his bridle. "How goes the fighting?"

He started to laugh, and ended with a hiccough. "Fighting? There was no fighting."

"How's that?" I persisted.

"We marched under the walls of the town and bade them to yield —and they did!" He broke off, swigged at his bottle, and winked at me. "Now, young sir, I must ride on with my dispatches."

"But why does not the army return?" I demanded, still holding his bridle.

"You cannot guess?" he flung back, with a soldier's contempt for one who does not understand military matters. "Why, the lads are plundering. What else? So would I be at the plunder, if I had not been ordered —"

I let him go, and with whip and spur I hastened my gray horse forward.

But I arrived too late, even had I had the power and knowledge to divert that misdeed.

Volterra gushed flame from within the ancient walls. Around the town capered the victorious troops, staggering under burdens of spoil, most of them drunker than the courier I had met. Even from afar I heard whooping laughter. The camp, a great field of tents beneath the hill which supported the ravished town, was almost deserted as I spurred in. By chance, I came almost at once to the commander's pavilion, and in front of it sat Federigo d'Urbino alone.

He slouched forward on his folding chair, his long, black-tufted chin clutched in a hard hand. His face was as somber as his armor was bright. I swung out of the saddle, and he glared up at me.

"Doubtless you bring dispatches from Florence," he barked. "Ride back and tell that blood-drinker, Lorenzo, that never will I draw sword for him again, not if he seeks to buy me with all the treasure of Croesus."

"What is this wild talk?" I demanded. "Is not this atrocity of your bidding?"

In my sick revulsion, I forgot that I called to account the first soldier of the Italian peninsula. But he only shook his head. "Nay, not my bidding.

Lorenzo's. I —I have a reputation as a gentleman and a merciful Christian."

"To be sure, it was Lorenzo's bidding," said a voice behind me, a voice that had a way of breaking in upon my conversations. "You, dear cousin, heard Lorenzo give me the message."

I spun, and thrust my angry face at Guaracco. "You dared order this pillage and destruction, as though you were Lorenzo's agent?"

"Aye, that," he seemed actually to boast, "and you can bear me witness with Messer Federigo. 'That physician is often most cruel —' "

"So you interpreted his thoughtless speech thus, you murderer!" I choked out, and from my scabbard I swept my blade. "Draw, before I cut you down!"

The red beard rustled in his old grin of mockery. "I have no sword, Leo," he said, as though chiding a boy. "I bear only — this." From under the fringe of his mantle peeped out that pistol I had helped him to invent.

Even so, I might have fallen upon him and forced him to shoot me; but Federigo d'Urbino, who did not recognize the deadly little weapon for what it was, sprang up and caught my arm.

"Do not add another murder to this massacre, young sir," he begged me. "Possibly Messer Guaracco did misunderstand. Yet —" He turned away. "Somehow I must stop these fiends at their hell's work."

Away he tramped. Left alone with me, Guaracco

stepped backward out of reach, pistol still leveled. "It is true that I urged Lorenzo's words upon the army, and it was none too squeamish to attack the town. I have even take a piece of loot myself. Come, I will show you."

At sometime during that speech he had thrust his other hand into view. Something gleamed softly and slyly between thumb and fingers —his great lustrous pearl, with its freight of spells.

I fought against its power as against a crushing weight, and indeed I did not lose my wits. But I grew weary and vague of thought, and let him coax me to sheathe my sword. "Come," he said again, and I went with him, slowly and a little drunkenly, to a tent not far from that of d'Urbino.

And there he showed me what he had seized from some Volterran shop or warehouse. It was a great soapy block of alum, reflecting subdued gray and blue lights as it lay upon a length of dirty canvas. It was almost exactly cubical, and a good yard along the edge.

"I knew that I must get hold of this very piece," Guaracco told me, "and so I passed on Lorenzo's orders. You must not blame me, Leo, if I show so much scientific zeal."

Some worse motive, I was sure, impelled him, but I gazed at the greasy-looking crystal. Its light seemed to drive away some of his spell. I saw even a gleam of hope.

The alum would allow completion of the time reflector. I would be quit of the Renaissance, its frustrations and fantasies. Above all, I would be quit of the abominable Guaracco.

XIV. ALMOST

Now, if ever, I can offer proof that this is not fiction. If it were, and I the hero, I would have tried to slaughter Guaracco then and there, in the camp before sacked, outraged Volterra. I would have set upon him, despite the triumphant display of the mammoth alum-crystal, despite his ready explanations, despite the pistol he kept in his hand. That would have been the honorable, the courageous and dramatic course.

But it happens that this story is true, and that I was and am of human clay. For two years, Guaracco had alternately intimidated and cajoled me, with judicious applications of hypnotic influence. My ultimate emotion was only of hopeful relief. If that be shameful, the reader may make the most of it.

We left the camp together, almost like friends, with peasants to attend a two-wheeled cart that bore the piece of alum. We did not go directly to Florence, but sought a rough winding road that took us around the town, and then to Guaracco's country house. There, with numerous helping hands, we placed the alum in the cellar workshop.

Guaracco knew more about grinding lenses than I did. Probably it was yet another Twentieth-Century science he had developed from his hypnotic inter-

views with my subconscious self. Besides, the alum
was a larger and softer piece of raw material than the
fragments of glass with which I had earlier tried to
work. In one day he roughed it into shape; and in
two more, with the help of the swordsmith, he made
of it a perfect double-convex lens. This, two feet in
diameter, was a grayly gleaming discus that dealt
weirdly with light.

The lens finished, we carried it upstairs, into that
same second-story chamber from which, in that Twentieth Century which now was to reclaim me, I had
vanished. It was the room where my friend Astley
must wait, at my direction, for my return.

I helped to bolt the rods into a framework, and to
lift into place Guaracco's battery, a massive but work-
manlike thing inside a bronze case worked over with
strange bas-reliefs. I think that case had come from
the Orient. The battery would do the work I had
done with many smaller cells in my own reflector.
Into sockets were fitted electric-light globes, most
cunningly wrought, again by Guaracco and in secret.

"They are not the best," he said.

"Will they serve?"

"I understand," and he smiled wispily, as always
when he referred to his findings through hypnosis,
"that an element called vanadium is the best for those
filaments inside."

"Vanadium is necessary," I remembered.

But he shook his head. "I substituted manganese. That, I have come to believe," and again his wispy smile turned upon me, "is almost as good. Obtainable, too, as vanadium is not." He looked upward with his lustrous eyes, as though in deep thought. "Did you not once predict, cousin, that a Genoese friend of the Vespucci family —Colombo is his name, I think —would discover a new land in the west?"

"I did."

"And is not vanadium plentiful in those latitudes? . . . Just so. But not readily to be found elsewhere. And so we must make manganese serve."

He studied the camera apparatus, slipped the lens of alum into place and clamped it tightly. Then he set the time guage. "First day of May, the year of our lord 1957. And there is, of course, that change in the calendar that you say will come." He changed the gauge a trifle. "Your friend is supposed to fetch a carcass from which your structure would be reapproximated by reflection, is it not so?" He straightened up from his tinkering. "Now, do you wish to say goodbye to Lisa?"

I had not forgotten Lisa; rather had I fought against thinking too much about this girl whom I refused as a gift from Guaracco, but to whom my heart turned whenever I would let it. I left the room immediately.

She lingered just outside the doorway in the upper

hall, dressed in a girdled gown of blue and with a cap upon her dark head. Her blue eyes gleamed like stars.

"Lisa," I said, in a voice I could not keep steady. "I have come to say —to say —"

"To say farewell?" Her hands rose to hide her face.

I could but catch her in my arms. I kissed her cheeks, and her tears were salt to my taste.

"Nay, do not cry," I whispered. "I beg you, do not cry. I swear to come back, to hurry back —"

"We shall not meet again," Lisa sobbed.

"I will come back," I vowed. "Since this second machine remains here, it will take us eventually into the age from whence I came."

"Us?" she repeated, trying to understand. "It will take us?"

"Lisa, I will rescue you from this century, and from the cruel and sorrowful world in which you have lived."

Guaracco cleared his throat. Still holding Lisa close, I looked to where his bearded head thrust around the edge of the door. "Forgive me for interrupting, but I must leave certain preparations in Lisa's hands. . . . Lisa, at this same time tomorrow, have brought into this room a slaughtered calf."

"Will you not see to that yourself?" I urged him.

"But I am seeing to it, Leo."

I kissed Lisa again, and walked into the room.

The power was turned on, the light gleaming blue-gray through the lens, the misty cloud hovering within the framework. Once passed, it would be 1957 beyond . . .

Then I saw that Guaracco was removing his last garment.

"What does this mean?" I demanded of him.

"I have decided to make the journey through time, instead of you."

"But I —" The words broke on my astonished lips.

"No arguments." He cut me off. "It is too late."

Before I could prevent him, he had fairly leaped into the midst of the framework, diving through that veil of fog.

For a moment I saw him there, as fragile as a man of soap bubbles, less than a ghost. I gazed, waiting for him to fade completely, but his substance did not vanish. He reeled, almost sank down, and then I saw his substance grow thick again, saw it take back his color. I saw the pink of his skin, the red of his beard, a writhing of his face.

He came staggering back out of the light, planting his feet to stay erect, as though he were on the deck of a rocking ship. He was still in his own age. The reflector was a failure.

I laughed triumphantly, and almost set myself to strike him. But he melted down upon a chair. So weak and wretched did he look that part of my fury departed from me. My clenched fists relaxed; I only stared and did not speak. For his attempt to trick me was of no use. He had not shoved himself into my own age at my expense.

He looked up and stared at me for long seconds.

"I can understand your feelings," he muttered at last, as humbly as a child caught in a jam closet. "Once more, I thought I had outwitted you. But I reap the reward of my own sinful vanity."

I was amazed. This was nothing like Guaracco. "Do not tell me that you repent."

His shaky fingers tried to wring the point of his beard. "Is it not permitted the proudest and foulest wrongdoer to say that he has done amiss?" he quavered, and his head bowed almost upon his bare, scrawny knees.

"You speak but to gain time for some other betrayal," I charged.

At that, he looked up. "Leo," he said, "let me make my poor excuses. My heart was full of zeal for what I should behold and learn, five centuries in the future. It would be to me what heaven is to the true and stainless believer. And now, and now, without even a glimpse—" He tottered to his feet, and held out a trembling hand. He seemed old and frail. "I beg you, do not laugh or reproach. I have been deceitful. Now let me make amends. We shall be true scientists and philosophers together. Will you not forgive me, Leo? Will you not take me at last as your friend?"

I could not exult over so patently broken an adversary, and his self-abnegation went far to disarm me. I took his hand. At once, he straightened his skinny body, and his voice and bearing recaptured some of the old assurance.

"That is better, Cousin Leo —for we are kinsmen in taste and in ambition, at least. What wonders shall we not perform together? The world will hear of us."

As he spoke, a commotion and the sound of an excited voice came from the floor below us. I, being dressed, ran out and down past Lisa.

Sandro Botticelli stood there inside the door. He was mud-spattered and panting as though he had ridden swiftly, and his plump, pleasant face was full of grave concern.

"Leo," he said as he spied me, "I risk my career, perhaps my life, in warning you. Fly, and at once."

"At once?" I echoed, scowling in amazement.

He gestured frantically. "Do not bandy words, man," he scolded me. "Begone, I say. Lorenzo has signed a writ for your arrest. You are doomed."

My mouth fell open, it seemed to me, a good twelve inches.

"It is because of what happened at Volterra," Botticelli plunged on. "That town was sacked because of you. Lorenzo wanted alum for his flying machine."

"Alum? Aye, we got alum —"

"But you did not make a flying machine with it, Leo. Criticism has flamed up over the treatment of the Volterrans, and Lorenzo needs a scapegoat. When

Guaracco's letter came, saying that you had used the alum for another purpose —"

"Guaracco!" I roared.

Of course, he had planned matters with his usual consistent genius for betrayal. He had meant to usurp my place at the time reflector, leaving me to imprisonment, perhaps to death on a trumped-up charge.

I started for the stairs again, for I wanted Guaracco's blood. But Botticelli leaped after me and caught my wrist. "I hear galloping hoofs, Leo. The officers are coming. Run, I say, run!"

At that moment the door burst open and two armed men rushed in.

XV. SANTI PELAGRINI

"You have come to arrest me?" I demanded of the men who so unceremoniously had entered. "Where is your warrant?"

"This is my warrant," said their chief, drawing his sword. "This, and the word of His Magnificence. He said you were to be taken, living or dead."

I wore not so much as a dagger for weapon. Resistance was useless. I could do nothing, except perhaps save poor Botticelli from possible punishment for riding to warn me. Therefore, I glowered at him. "You see that you will get no reward, after all," I taunted him with simulated irony. "These gentlemen will take me before Lorenzo, not you."

"How —" he began, but I interrupted.

"It is well for you that they came. Your effort to arrest me might have ended with your getting hurt. I advise you to stick to paint daubing, and not to play catchpole again."

He stared at me in pained surprise, then grateful understanding peeped through. I walked out, closely guarded by my captors, and was directed to mount a spare horse. Then we started, but upon a road that led away from Florence.

"Did not His Magnificence send you to seize me?"

I asked. "Then take me before him, that my case may be heard."

"Your case has been heard already," I was told.

We went southeast, mile after mile, leaving the good main road for shorter and rougher stretches. I asked where we were going and what my fate would be, and was bidden to save my breath. We stopped that night at a little house, where a grape grower sold us bread and cheese and wine, and gave us sleeping room in his front chamber. I lay in front of the fireplace, and my companions stood armed watch over me by turns.

At midmorning of the next day, we rode into the seaport of Rimini, and straight to the stone wharfs. The chief of our party sent a messenger to call ashore the captain of a small lateen-rigged vessel riding close in at anchor. He talked aside with this captain, and showed him an official-looking document. Then I was taken from my horse and led forward.

"Go you with this shipmaster," the chief officer ordered me.

I protested loudly, and nobody replied. The captain brought two sailors with knives in their hands, and these conducted me to a skiff, in which I was rowed out, helped to the half-deck, and placed in a closetlike compartment off the captain's cabin. We sailed at noon.

The captain brought me food, and deigned to tell me a little of what was happening to me.

"You are sent to be imprisoned, sir," he said, "at the *Fortaleza degli Santi Pelagrini* —the Fortress of the Holy Pilgrims."

I had never heard of that fortress, and said so.

"It is a great service to heaven," the captain elaborated. "Holy men built it, two good centuries gone, for an abbey. But the heathen Turk, who flouts true belief and seeks to conquer us all, has taken the coastline on the far side of the Adriatic Sea, save only that blessed fortress."

"Who garrisons it?" I asked.

"Who but the Holy Pilgrims themselves? They hold their own, in the very teeth of false Mohammed."

He told me more about the order of the Holy Pilgrims. They were military monks, not powerful or high-born, as were the Templars or the Knights of St. John, but simple commoners, sworn to the church and armed and trained to fight. As he described them, they had originated as a band of peasants who, coming to Jerusalem at the height of the Crusades, had been inspired to forsake the world and enter the church. After the ousting of the Christians from Palestine, they had survived as a brotherhood and had fought on; and now they stubbornly defended the island on which their fortress-priory stood, not many miles off the coast occupied by Moslems.

And these were to be my jailers. It did me no good to protest my innocence and my right to a trial.

Lorenzo's anger, stimulated by the lies of Guaracco, had driven him to doom me to imprisonment without benefit of a hearing. He, or any other ruler of the time, was able to do just such a thing, putting a man away as easily as he might put away a book or a suit of worn clothes. I could be thankful that he had not ordered me killed. Or could I?

Five days we sailed before a light breeze, south and slightly eastward across the waters of the Adriatic. I was not permitted to go on deck, but there was a latticed port in my cabin, and I saw as quickly as any lookout the two rakish galleys, with crescent-blazoned banners, that on the fifth day gave us chase.

For a while it was a close race, and I wondered if I might soon exchange my enforced idleness in the barred cabin for labor at the oar of a Turkish galley. Then guns spoke from somewhere to our front, a cheer went up from our sailors, and we drew near the defending shores of the island where stood the Fortress of the Holy Pilgrims.

I was allowed at last to come on deck. I saw the island as a rocky protuberance from the blue ocean, its flattish top green with growth, and with but a single landing place —an arm of the sea, extending almost to the foot of the great square-towered castle of gray stone that dominated all points of the rock. A boat put out from the sailing vessel, with myself, the captain, and sailors to row and guard. Looking back to sea, I could make out, far off, the sullen Turkish galleys.

We came to the mouth of the inlet, and found that it bore two great lumpish towers of masonry, one at either brink, for the stretching of a chain, if the enemy were to be kept from sailing in. A simple enough device, and I remembered as I looked at the towers that a chain system like this at West Point had kept the British ships from sailing up the Hudson during our Revolutionary War.

A skiff came forward to meet us; it was rowed by two tanned, shaven-headed men in black serge robes, while a third stood upright with his foot upon the thwart, a crossbow ready in his hands. Its cord was drawn back, and a bolt lay ready in the groove.

"Who are you?" called the crossbowman in a clear, challenging voice.

"A Christian vessel, with a message and a prisoner for you," yelled back the captain.

A jerk of the crossbowman's shaven skull granted us leave to enter the sheltered inlet. As we came close to the skiff, I saw that each of the monks wore a symbol on his breast, a black cross outlined in white, with a white cockleshell in the center, emblematic of the church and pilgrimage. Side by side, the two open boats rowed to a dock of massive mortared stones, and we landed.

One of the monk-oarsmen went swiftly ahead with

the papers the captain had brought, while the rest of
us mounted more leisurely to the paved slope that
led to the great gate of the castle. I looked right and
left, upon the outdoors which I might well be leaving
for a term of years or forever.

There were goats in a little herd; a series of rock-
bordered fields, where monks with looped-up gowns
hoed crops, apparently of beans and barley; an arbor
of grapevines. And, at the few spots where the steep
shores relented enough to allow men to reach the
seaside, parties of gowned fishermen seined for sar-
dines and mullet.

The big gateway of colossal timbers, fastened with
ancient copper bolts, stood open, allowing us to pass
through an inner courtyard. Just within stood a row
of black-robed men, armed with spears, apparently
taking part in a military drill of most unpriestly snap
and precision. They were all tanned, lean and hard-
faced, and handled their weapons with the disciplined
readiness of trained soldiers, which indeed they were.
Into the castle hall we went, then down a corridor,
and to a plain, windowless cell, lighted by a candle.

"Father Agostino!" respectfully called the monk
who had been our conductor.

Someone stood up behind the plain table in the
office. He was a gaunt, fierce man who wore a robe
and symbol in no way differing from the others; yet
I knew instantly that here was the master of the
fortress.

His shoulders rose high and broad, so that he seemed a great black capital Y of a man. His face, dark as a Moor's, was seamed and cross-hatched with scars. His nose had been smashed flat by some heavy blow; the right corner of his mouth was so notched that a tooth gleamed through at us, and over his left eye was tied a black patch. But the other eye quested over us with stern appraisal.

The monk offered the letter that the captain had brought. Father Agostino opened it and read it quickly, then spoke, in a deep voice of practiced command. "Go, Brother Pietro, and fetch Giacopo the clerk. He shall write to Lorenzo de' Medici that this prisoner shall be held here as he desires."

The monk saluted and walked away, as briskly as a well-trained orderly. Father Agostino spoke to the captain. "Will you partake of our humble hospitality, my son?"

"Gladly will I, Holy Father," was the captain's reply. "I dare not leave your anchorage and the shelter of your guns until yonder sea-roving heathen dogs depart, in any case."

The notched mouth smiled, and looked harder for that smile. "Nay, they shall depart within the hour. Our own warcraft will see to that. We have two armed boats of our own, and not a Holy Pilgrim of us but is worth three of the best of those Turkish pirates, whose feet have fast hold of hell. I shall order a party out to lash them away."

He came forth from the office, and I noticed that he limped slightly, and that around his lean middle, outside the gown, was belted a cross-hilted sword in a battered sheath.

"Is this the prisoner?" he asked, fixing his single eye upon me. "Prisoner, I do call upon you to repent your sin."

"Most freely do I repent all sins that lie upon my soul, Holy Father," I replied at once. "But of the sin with which I stand charged, I cannot repent, since of it I am entirely innocent. The guilty are those who falsely swore against me."

"He is a lying dog," grumbled the captain, but I thought that the chopped face and single eye of the prior of the Holy Pilgrims were lighted up, as though in quiet approval of my boldness.

Another monk arrived, with a sword at his hip and a half-pike upon his shoulder. At Father Agostino's order, he marched me away, upstairs and along a gallery.

We came into a corridor lined on either side with locked doors, and heavy with a musty, sweaty prison smell. A burly black-gowned porter unlocked a door of heavy planking and pushed me inside.

My cell was some six feet by ten, with a wooden cot at the rear. Above this was a window, not more than a foot square, and defended by two crossbars. The walls were all of uneven cut stone, the mortar scraped away from around each to the depth of a full inch—

the work, as I judged, of many an idle prisoner. There was a straw mattress, a stool, a wooden refuse bucket, an earthen jug for water. The door that clanged shut behind me had a sliding wooden panel, through which food could be passed to me, or slops poured forth into a gutter outside.

When I stretched, my hands could touch the ceiling overhead. And when I knelt on the straw mattress, I saw that my window was a tunnel through seven feet of solid wall. I looked out upon a sandy shelf, and beyond that to the sea.

This was to be my home, for heaven and Lorenzo de' Medici knew how long.

XVI. CAPTIVITY

For the next six years I remained locked in a cell,
save for the brief moments I spent in moving from
one prison to another.

I knew of no passage of time except by the shifting
of the sunlighted patch on my wall opposite the little
window, and by the arrival, each noon, of coarse food
in a wooden plate and water in a leather mug. This
provision, rude but plentiful, I divided into three
meals. It was the same fare, I make no doubt, as that
of the monks who served as my jailers.

On the biggest stone in my wall I scratched the
date of my imprisonment. I recognized Sundays because on those days I received a cup of sour wine,
and could hear, beyond the door and the corridor,
the muffled intoning of a mass. Then I would make
a mark under the date, to denote the passing of a
week.

Those weekly marks added into months, and the
months into years.

Well aware of the breakdown of prisoners' minds,
I fought to stay rational. I found myself pacing up
and down, like a frantic beast in a cage. To break
myself of that unprofitable habit, I spent hours at
calisthenics, which did keep me fairly fit. Too, I

sketched and drew on the stones with bits of burnt wood, and sometimes incised pictures with the steel tongue of my belt buckle.

Barely realizing that I did so, I fashioned from memory a portrait of Lisa as last I had seen her, with a face full of gentle sadness at the thought of my vanishing through time. I began with deeply scratched outlines, and shadowed and refined the whole with soot and charcoal.

"Now the saints look down upon us!" cried an armed monk, entering on one of the tours of inspection. "Young man, you have made the blessed Virgin, the Mother of God, there on your wall."

He stepped to another part of the cell to look at the picture, and crossed himself.

"Let me move where I will, her eyes look at me," he said. "It is a miracle, perhaps."

When he had gone, I gazed at the face I had drawn. I stepped to a far corner, looked again, then shifted my position. The monk had spoken truth; without meaning to do so, I had so drawn Lisa that her eyes followed me. It was a quiet comfort to my lonely soul.

But hardly ever did anyone so speak to me, not even the monk who thrust my daily ration in at the slide-covered hole in the door. I had long, long hours of privacy. In the summer of 1474, my second in the cell, I decided that escape need not be an impossibility.

Laboriously I detached a stout leg of my bedstead,

and with this as a lever, I worried the crossbars out of my window. They had been set in mortar, and had sharp points. Using one as a chisel, I began stealthily to widen the narrow aperture. Each night I worked thus, and lightly wedged the bars back at dawn, to deceive any visitor who might come.

After a month, I felt that my digging was sufficient; but it was not. I tried to wriggle through that tunnel of a window, and became wedged helplessly in it. There I was forced to remain until a goatherd, chasing his charges around the walls, happened to spy my mournfully protruding head. It took two muscular friars to drag me back into the cell, and I was marched between them to stand before Father Agostino.

The prior of the Holy Pilgrims spoke sadly concerning my prideful and rebellious nature, urged me to pray for forgiveness and a softer heart, then pronounced a sentence of a term on bread and water, and twenty lashes with a knotted cord.

"I shall die before I am flogged," I said at once.

A monk appeared with the cord and struck as with a burning wire across my shoulders. Rage exploded within me like gunpowder. I wrenched free from the two who held me, tackled my flogger, and threw him heavily.

My fingers dug into his throat, and then half a dozen of the Holy Pilgrims fell upon me and dragged me roughly from my victim.

Father Agostino had watched the incident with an appraising light in his single eye. "You refuse, young man, to be corrected," he said coldly.

"Keep your lash for slaves," I retorted passionately. "You can kill me, but you cannot whip me."

To my considerable surprise, he nodded slowly and understandingly. His eye seemed to dance a trifle, and he smiled, revealing other sharp white teeth than the one that glittered through the notch in his lip.

"Well, well, be it so," he granted, actually with kindness in his tone. "I remit the flogging. But you must be closer penned. Brethren, put him in the cell below his old one."

They did so. The new prison was smaller, and for bed had only a wooden shelf under the window, spread with musty straw. The window itself was cross-barred, and looked out upon a face of hewn rock. This part of the fortress was below ground, and a foot-wide trench was all that gave me air and light. Digging my way free was out of the question.

More gloom settled closely around my burdened soul, but I recognized that I had gained one advantage, the stern and almost approving respect of Father Agostino. He, a natural fighter, admired the fighting spirit in another.

To him, I sent request for a lamp and pen and paper. These were given me, and I had some surcease from ennui by writing and drawing. Among other things, I set down in outline most of the story told here in full. That outline is spread before me as I write these words, and is a check against my often untrustworthy memory.

I kept up my exercises, too, shadowboxed on occasion, and in this cell, as in the other, achieved a portrait of Lisa.

But I still had many hours in which to meditate upon the injustice of Lorenzo's decree that thus had buried me alive, and upon the things I would do to Guaracco if ever I came within clutch of him. Of Lisa I dreamed, fondly and sadly, night after night.

In that fall of 1474, and again two years later, attacks in force were made against the Fortress of the Holy Pilgrims. There was deafening cannon-fire from the stronghold, and more in reply from ships, and once an effort was made to storm us. I could hear commotion, fierce yells, the clash of steel against steel. In the end, as I was able to judge, the austere soldiers of the church repulsed their enemies, and for a day the battered castle rang with chanted paeans of grateful praise to heaven for the victory.

I grew to have a philosophic sympathy with those jailers of mine. They imprisoned me because of an agreement with Lorenzo. They confined me closely because I had forced them to do that. If my food was plain, my bed hard, so also were theirs. And for the rest, they were tireless workers, sincere worshippers and sturdy fighters. The world, I came to feel, was crowded with worse people.

Thus I reasoned, but still I must struggle desperately to remain sane. I tried to remember *The Prisoner of Chillon,* which might offer one or two stanzas of comfort for the captive, but it would not come to mind. In any case, Lord Byron would not write it for a good three hundred and forty years.

In this second cell, I remained utterly alone. No monk entered to inspect, and the jailer only glanced through the slide in the door. These matters heartened me to new thoughts of escape.

The spring of 1477 saw yet another attack by enemies, a stronger and more stubborn effort to capture the Fortress of the Holy Pilgrims. I could hear the battering of a wall close to me, and the overthrow of part of it. So hot was the fight, so narrowly balanced the issue for an hour, that the jailer-monk rushed from the corridor outside my cell to help defend the ramparts. During his absence, with the din of conflict around me, I had time to do a thing I had long planned.

The lamp that lighted me was an iron saucer with a central clip to hold aloft the wick. I ignited straw and chips gouged from my bed and, holding one edge of the lamp saucer in a fold of my ragged doublet, contrived to heat the opposite edge red-hot. Then, with a piece of stone for a hammer and the bed shelf for an anvil, I pounded, reheated, and pounded again, until I beat that segment of the rim into a knifelike edge. After the battle the jailer returned, too late to hear my noisy labors. And I began to whittle at my wooden door.

The planks were thick, and seasoned almost as hard as iron; but I persevered all that stifling summer. I counted myself lucky when, between one dawn and the next, I shaved away as much as a double handful of splinters.

Boresome it was, and eventually it seemed heartbreaking, for my first burrowing brought me through the thick wood to metal. I dug at another place, hoping to avoid such a barrier, but I found more—more, that is, of the same sheet.

Eventually I had removed much of the door's inner surface, and found myself confronted with a copper plate, a central layer, probably with as much wood outside as I had already hewed away inside. My tappings and proddings convinced me that the rest of the door was solid and massive, except for the small slide-covered opening.

I cursed and sulked, and wished for cutting tools. The jagged shred of glass I used for an occasional shave was far from adequate. Even if I could have found or made file, chisel or drill, I would not have dared use them, for the noise would attract the guards. What then?

Acid came to mind. The stones of my cell were volcanic; perhaps they contained sulphides and, if properly burnt and distilled, might yield sulphuric acid. But I had no equipment for that. I shrugged and shook my head, grown shaggy with the years. I must consider, I knew, not how to procure the best acid, but the most available.

Chilly autumn was upon us, and the sharp, strong wine was served daily instead of on Sunday only. Tasting it, I became inspired once more.

When my next food was brought, I pleaded for a little vinegar to treat a chest ailment. It was brought me in a saucer, and I steeped in it some of the shavings whittled from the door. When they seemed sour enough, I placed them at the bottom of my wooden slop bucket. Into this, day after day, I trickled my allowance of wine. It produced a greater quantity of excellent vinegar, and after tasting it, I felt sure of my acid.

Painfully scrabbling with a spoon in the trench outside my window, I secured enough clay to mix with water and fashion into clumsy basins and jars. These I cautiously hardened in another fire of straw and chips, and employed to store my vinegar as I manufactured it.

Of more clay I constructed a really workable distillery. It was a narrow-mouthed vase or bottle, suspended above a fire which I fed with splinters from the door and the bed. As winter came on, I heated vinegar in this, and the vapor passed through a hollow reed which I cooled with bits of ice from just outside my barred window. The condensed drops I caught in another cup. They proved to be strongly acid, perhaps enough for my purpose.

These labors lasted for months. I speak of them here but briefly, saying nothing of the trial and error, the ludicrous failures and the chance successes that alternately dashed and encouraged me. At length, well after Christmas of 1477, I began my attack on the copper plate that held me from freedom.

At the height of my forehead, and again at the height of my knee, I built clay troughs against the metal. These I filled, and kept filled, with my acid. At first, the action proved slight, and I increased it by the addition of salt from my food. This gave me a crude form of hydrochloric acid, which achieved a reckonable effect on the copper. Again and again I scraped away the particles of corroded metal and replenished the supply of salted acid. I wrought for more months, and finally I was rewarded by the eating away of the final layers of copper along those two narrow lines.

The perpendicular acidulation was more difficult, but I managed by molding two clay tubes at the sides of the door, open at the top, rather like the covered tunnels built by tropical ants. These extended from the upper cut in the copper to the lower, and I filled them again and again, occasionally pulling them away to dig at the digested copper, then building them afresh for new attacks.

Here, too, I was successful. One day in February I was able to lift away the whole rectangle of metal within the compass of my four channels so painfully cut by acid. Beyond was more thick wood, but, heartened by my triumph, I scraped and chiseled day after day until the door was almost as thin as pasteboard, although to the outside view it would appear as solid as ever.

At midday of April 16, 1478, I made my bid for escape.

The attendant came to my door and pushed aside the panel, then stooped to thrust in my food. I had been waiting for an hour, tense and ready. When I heard him there outside, I sprang, bursting through the thin wood like a clown through a paper hoop.

Landing on the monk's unsuspecting back, I whipped an arm beneath his chin, shutting off his breath. He could not cry out or draw a weapon, and his struggles availed nothing. I throttled him until his limbs grew slack, then let him sink to the stone floor. I stripped off his robe, donned it and pushed him, still senseless, through the smashed door to my cell.

Then I pulled the cowl over my face and headed down the corridor, his keys in my hand. I unlocked the door at the end of the passage, mounted a flight of steps, and traversed another corridor, with measured tread, as though deep in meditation.

None challenged me. I came into the main hall, saw the open doorway to the courtyard. Beyond that would be the open, the beach, boats. I could get into one and row away, and others would think I was a brother going to fish. Once free of the fortress, I would seek land, even among the Turks. Already I savored freedom.

Then a dry voice spoke at my elbow. "You pass me without saluting."

Father Agostino had fallen into step beside me. I lifted a hand to my hooded brow, and his single eye fastened upon it.

"How white is your flesh, brother. I thought that every monk of our order was tanned by labor in God's sunlight. Who are you?"

There was nothing for it but battle, and I wheeled and grappled him.

Surprise was on my side. I tripped him and fell heavily upon him. But that old priest-soldier, lame and half-blind, was as strong as I, and as fierce. I clutched and pressed his throat, but he caught my little fingers in his hard hands, bent them painfully backward until I let go of his stringy throat, then shifted his grip so that his thumbs drove into the nerves at the inner sides of my biceps.

I rolled free of him, and we came to our feet together. I struck him heavily on the jaw, and his one eye blinked, but he did not stagger or flinch. Strongly clutching me around the waist, he drove me back against a wall.

There he held me, despite my pummeling fists in

his face, while a dozen monks, swords and axes in hand, rushed in from all directions. Again I tripped Father Agostino and threw him, but then they had me by the arms and body and dragged me away. Father Agostino rose, dabbing at a trickle of blood from his scarred nose. He panted and grinned, as though he had enjoyed the struggle.

"Here's a stout sinner," he growled. "Never did the blessed angel clip Father Jacob more strongly. Thank you for the bout, my son; I sorrow that your strength is not employed to the good of men instead of to their injury. Take him to my office."

I was taken there, and kept under close guard, while the prior stumped away to investigate. He returned after half an hour and dismissed the guards, but kept his dagger drawn lest I attack him again.

"I am amazed at the cunning and courage and labor of your attempt," he said frankly. "How did you manage to cut through the door, copper and all?"

I described my methods, and he listened with interest. Several times he asked me to explain the making of acid or the action of it on copper. At length he gave me that harsh, approving smile.

"You have science and inspiration, my son. How great would be your works if they were turned to honest and godly use."

"Being held prisoner, I can turn them only to efforts at escape," I replied.

"Aye, but your months of toil, so brilliantly

planned and so wearily pursued, have come to naught within minutes. A tragedy." Father Agostino paused and meditated. Then: "How then, my son, if I gave you freedom?"

"Freedom?" I echoed him unbelievingly.

"Within limits, of course. But if I took you from your cell and let you live among the brothers? You could work more science, with true materials to aid you instead of those makeshifts." He gazed at me, calculatingly, wonderingly. "I am serious. Say but one word, swear that you will not seek to flee from us —"

"Father, I am sorry," I broke in, "but I cannot so doom myself."

"Doom yourself? But you are now held by iron bars and guards."

"And under a false charge, brought against me by the vilest of knaves," I rejoined. "I thank you, good Father, for your offer, which you made in honest kindness. But I live only to escape and to avenge myself. I cannot give you my parole."

He shook his scarred head, and I thought he sighed in disappointment. Then he stepped to the door. "Hither, some of you," he commanded. "We must find this fellow a stronger prison still."

At that moment, a new figure pushed through the circle of black gowns, a man in the dress of the world, all particolored hose and plum-purple mantle, with a gay beard and curling locks.

"Surely," said he, "this is Messer Leo, the artist and scientist, who is held captive here by order of Lorenzo the Magnificent."

"Aye, that," nodded Father Agostino. "You know him, my son?"

"I have seen him in Florence," was the reply. "Where does he go now?"

"To an oubliette, I am afraid. From there he will need wings to rise."

Two of the armed brothers had torn away my disguising robe, and now they marched me down steps, more steps, to a level of natural rock where no light shone save a torch in an iron clamp. One of them hoisted a great iron trapdoor. I looked down into a bottle-shaped pit, at least twelve feet deep.

At that very moment, the upper levels of the castle wakened to noise —a blown trumpet, a chorus of yells. The two monks turned to look. I tightened my sinews for a last desperate fight against them, before I might be hurled into that tomblike prison. A flying figure appeared on the stairs.

"The infidel Turks! Their galleys blacken the seas! Come, every Holy Pilgrim, to the defense!"

"As soon as we lower this captive into —" began one of my warders.

"Nay!" A bearded face looked over the black-clad shoulder of the news-bringer, and I recognized the visitor who had appeared in the upper hall. "Bring him along. He will help fight."

"Well thought of," came the deep voice of Father Agostino, higher on the stairs. "Free every captive, every man who can bear arms. Let them fight for life!"

We all raced up the steps together.

XVII. DEFENSE OF THE FORTRESS

Mounting swiftly to battlements around the upper
wall of the castle, we could see that the ocean was
indeed full of craft. There were painted galleys, a
full dozen of them, many smaller feluccas, and open
rowboats swarming as thickly as a school of mullet.
Drums resounded from the larger ships, and horns.
Our own bugles brayed back defiantly.

Father Agostino was rasping orders like any seasoned captain.

"Man and load each gun," he commanded. "Line
the walls, keep lookout for where they may seek to
land." His eye found me. "Ha, you wrestler, can you
use a sword?" He motioned to an aide, who thrust a
hilt into my hand. "You have fought your fellow-
Christians overlong. Fight now against false infidels."

I shifted the weapon to my left fist, and tried its
balance. At a nearby rampart stood the man who had
recommended my joining the defenders, and toward
him I made quick steps.

"I do not know you, sir, though you say you know
me," I said. "My thanks for saving me from that
spider's hole into which they would have thrown
me."

"We will speak more of it anon." He pointed to

173

where, inside the little harbor, lay a trim sailing vessel among the boats of the Holy Pilgrims. "Yonder is my craft, and upon it a fair lady who must not set foot on this monk-owned island. I pray heaven naught befalls either of them."

"Nay," I comforted him. "See where the brothers string a heavy chain across the mouth of the inlet. That will prevent the approach of any enemy ships, and it seems that they wish to storm us from this other side."

Beyond the battlements, the wall dropped straight to the sea and had been badly damaged, perhaps in the fight a spring before, when I had heard the loud breaking of stones. The brothers had patched it with broken masonry and spaded earth, faced it with timbers and logs; but it was still the weak spot of the defenses.

Even the stone flooring at the top had collapsed and was mended with planking; instead of an adequate parapet, a work of earth-filled goatskins had been laid in and topped by a great log, nearly a hundred feet long. From this log ran back crosspieces, lashed on as slanting braces.

Here, even as we came upon the scene, the fire from the Turkish galleys was concentrated. Round shot tore holes in the goatskins and let out cascades of dirt, while a blizzard of arrows and sling-pebbles picked off such of the brothers as looked above the log-topped parapet. The others crouched low to save themselves.

"They will seek to carry us from this quarter," announced Father Agostino, limping across to the log.

His gown, kilted up for more active movement, showed great steel greaves upon his lanky shins, and he had thrown back his cowl to don a plumeless helmet. A bolt from a crossbow struck his shoulder, but glanced away from the steel cuirass under his robe.

"Aye," he called, "here they come, a hell's spawn of boats, under the fire of their fellows. Keep down, brethren, until they mount our wall. Then the fire must slacken, and we will meet these unbelievers with an argument they will understand." Drawing his sword, he spat between lean hand and worn hilt.

I dared expose myself to peer over the log. A shoal of boats swept swiftly toward us from the galleys, boats filled with howling and gesticulating Turks. I saw the glitter of their mail, the curves of their flourished scimitars, the upward jut of spiked helmets from their turbans. A moment later, a jagged little stone sang upward and against my forehead, slung, like David's pebble, from a sling. Like Goliath, I fell sprawling on my back, half-dazed, and almost dropping my sword.

Father Agostino leaned farther from his point of vantage, careless of the rain of missiles. "They raise

ladders!" he roared. "Here they mount!" He gestured
with his sword and his free hand. "Strike, brethren,
for the true faith!"

I got back to my feet somewhat groggily, and
watched as a line of black-robes moved swiftly and
purposefully over the planked-in floor, swords and
axes and halberds at the ready. The sound of firing
had ceased from galleyward, even as Father Agostino
had predicted. From below rose a concerted, yodeling
cry.

"*Ulululallahuakbar!*"

It was a prolonged bellow, of challenge and of
profession. Then the outer side of our great log was
lined with turbaned, bearded faces.

The storming party was upon us, eager for trouble.
Nor could they have come to a better place to seek it.

The Holy Pilgrims hurled themselves upon the
attackers, calling upon the names of all the saints in
the calendar, and hewing and thrusting like fiends
instead of clergymen. At their head, and in the
hottest press, hobbled Father Agostino, his straight
sword playing like the tongue of a great deadly snake
against a whole forest of scimitars.

I moved in his direction, and well for him that I
did. While his point wedged in the neckbone of one
adversary, another charged close and, catching him
by a fold of his gown, slashed a scimitar viciously at
his head.

The blow was turned by Father Agostino's helm,

but its force staggered him, and a second blow beat him to his knee. With a whoop, the Turk lifted his blade for a third and finishing cut, but then I hurled myself between, my own steel forestalling the scimitar.

The Turk was a deep-chested fellow, brown as chocolate, with mad foam on his black beard. *"Ya Nazrani!"* he raged at me, and struck.

But I was more than his match; my first parry extended into a slicing lunge that laid open his face. My second bit into the side of his neck. He collapsed, bleeding from nose and mouth, to die even as I turned to find another foe.

The surviving Turks reeled back, whipped along by the savage garrison. They tumbled down their ladders and rowed hurriedly away in their boats, with a new storm of shot and arrows to batter them.

Father Agostino was up again, glancing around to estimate the situation.

"We have suffered sorely," he judged, "but they suffered worse. What says Holy Writ? 'Blessed be the Lord my strength, who teacheth my hands to war, and my fingers to fight.'" He turned his eye on me. "Thanks for the rescue, my son. You smote like an angel of the Lord. Yet I make no doubt that, with heaven's help, I could have risen and overthrown him. Whence will come the next assault?"

We found out soon enough. Three great galleys swung away from the fleet, to move against the mouth of our inlet. The crews of the guns leveled in that direction toiled and fired madly, but could not drive them back. The galleys drew close, and a great throng of little black figures dived overside and struck out for the inlet.

"They carry axes!" cried the black-bearded stranger who had befriended me. "They will attack the chain! If it is cut, they will come in and seize our ships!"

"A sortie!" yelled Father Agostino. "Out, brethren, and meet them in the water!"

He led the rush downward himself, leaving only the armed prisoners and a dozen black-robes to hold the upper ramparts. We watched, fascinated, as the monks burst from the great gate and charged down to the water's edge. Some of them fell, shot by crossbowmen from the galleys, but the greater part splashed into the water and swam to meet the Turks. There was a fierce, clumsy melee in the waves that lapped along either side of the chain.

"The brethren triumph," exulted a monk at my side. "Look, the forgotten of God are retreating — swimming away."

"And more readily than I had hoped," I replied, thinking of the previous stubborn assault. "Stay, brother, what if it were a false attack to withdraw us from our own defense?"

Even as I spoke, I saw that the galleys were pulling away with all their oars, skirting the rocks narrowly and speeding around to the point from which the earth-mended wall had been stormed.

"Rally, friends! Rally!" I howled, and rushed across to the log upon the rampart of goatskins.

It was as I had been inspired to guess. The sea was full of boats again, scores of them, rowing furiously to the new attack. A spatter of shafts and shot made the few of us who were left put our heads down.

"What is to be done?" demanded a wild-eyed monk with a smear of blood upon his chin. "See, their whole force comes to this side, more than the first time —their rush will beat us back before our comrades return from the chain to defend the castle!"

"Stand to the rampart! Hurl down their ladders!" stoutly urged an armed captive.

But as he leaned forward to suit action to word, a crossbow bolt whacked into him, and he crumpled limply across the log. The rest of us crouched down, sword in hand, determining to die hard.

I knelt beside one of the great lashed crosspieces that propped the long log as a coping. It was none too firm, that crosspiece, I judged. And again I was inspired.

"Hear ye all!" I cried at the top of my voice. "We can save ourselves. Form in parties by these crosspieces, clutch them in your arms. If we bear with all our strength at once, it will force the great log outward and forward!"

"To what good?" demanded someone.

"To overthrow the ladders, as we cannot do when they shoot at us. Do not argue, my friends, but do as I say!"

There was no time or hope for any other plan. In a trice we formed in half a dozen knots, all stooping or squatting or kneeling, our weapons flung down and our arms wrapped around the cross-timbers.

Roars and execrations rang from beneath us, where the ladders were being hoisted from the boat bottoms to give access to our fortress. I felt my heart race like the roll of a drum, but kept my eyes steadily on the parapet, where the upright ends of the ladders lifted themselves into view.

"*Allahuakbar!*" thundered the war cry, and again a row of heads shot up above the log.

"Now!" I croaked my loudest, and taxed all my muscles to drag forward on the timber I clutched.

There was a concerted grunt from all of us as we bore mightily against the log. And, as I had dared to hope, the mass of timber slid gratingly forward, as a drawer slides from a bureau. With it swayed the storming ladders, so precariously balanced, and toppled over backward in a rank. A single concerted shriek assailed heaven from the many throats of those who were suddenly hurled back, down, among the boats and rocks and into the surf.

Dragging back our timber defense, we cheered each other in wild and thankful triumph.

That unexpected reverse gave the Moslems pause —a blessed, blessed pause for us, enough for the return and remarshaling of the party that had gone out with Father Agostino. The prior heard someone gasp out the story of our own success, and he clapped my shoulder with a hard, dripping hand. "You have saved this holy fortress, and if it were but in my power to set you free —"

He stumped away to thunder new orders. I stood alone for the moment, then a hand clutched my sleeve. It was the hand of the bearded man whose name I did not know, but who knew me; the man whose boat was in the little harbor below. "Come, Messer Leo," he said under his breath. "If the good Father cannot set you free, I can."

"How?" I demanded.

He did not pause to reply, but drew me to the stairs and down. We went unchallenged through the lower parts of the castle, and came to the gate. He lifted the huge latch, and we stepped outside.

"See," he said, "the Turkish boats have all gone around to the other side, hoping to make good that assault which you foiled. Now is my time to depart. I have too fast a ship for any heathen pirate to catch, and I will take you along."

I was too amazed and thankful to speak. A moment later we had hurried down, sprung aboard his half-decked sailing vessel, and were headed out for that quarter of the sea just now unguarded and unobserved by either Holy Pilgrim or infidel Turk, the sea beyond which lay the Italy I had quitted as a captive six years before.

XVIII.   RETURN TO FLORENCE

As soon as my feet were on the deck, my enigmatic rescuer hustled me into the cabin, where he left me alone. I heard his shouted orders on deck, heard the creaking of ropes, felt the ship move. We sailed out, unchallenged and unchecked, and headed northwest. Behind me, I heard the muffled commotion of a fresh attack on the fortress, but we were not pursued.

After some time, the master of the vessel reappeared. He offered me a razor, with which I thankfully took my first decent shave since I had left Florence. A mirror showed me my face, smooth again, but no longer fresh and boyish.

My brow was cleft with a frown mark. My nose and chin had hardened, and my eyes blazed as with challenge and truculence. My hair, grown long, showed threads of gray. Over one temple rose a purple bump, where the Turkish slinger had struck me. Mine was not a pretty face.

"May I give you these clothes?" asked my rescuer.

I pulled on dark green hose, a velvet doublet, and pointed shoes. Then I gazed in surprise at the cloak he offered, a cloak of Florentine scarlet.

"Why, it is mine!" I exclaimed. "I wore it before. It was given me by —"

"Aye, by Guaracco," he supplied. "I received it from him."

"But Guaracco caused me to be imprisoned," I protested.

"And now he causes you to be freed," was the answer. "He knew, through his spies, that the Turks made ready to attack. He arranged that I come to the fortress in good time for that event."

"To help me escape?" I prompted.

"Aye, that. It took but a word in good season to draw you out of your cell and into the ranks of the defenders. After that —but have patience. You shall know all anon. Stay in this cabin, for it would be ill if any sailor saw you and gabbled too much."

And so I stayed in the cabin that day and for some days following. The master brought me food with his own hands, and talked to me pleasantly, though he would not answer questions about why he had come to rescue me. At last, on the morning of April 25, we docked. Peeping through a porthole, I watched the mariners tie us up to the pilings.

I raked the shore with my eyes, on the lookout for Guaracco. My heart stewed with the accusations I would hurl at him. As I rehearsed them under my breath, the master of the vessel entered. "Here is a fellow-passenger of yours, whom at last I am able to bring to you."

With him appeared a slender figure, cloaked and masked as at a carnival. Saying no word, this figure handed me a folded and sealed parchment. On the outside was written:

> This to the hand of my Kinsman Leo,
>> Quickly,
>> Quickly,
>> Quickly.

Wondering, I broke the seals and read:

My dear cousin and partner:

Do not think me neglectful if I have left you, like a dagger in a sheath, until the time was ripe to use you for both our profits. For the ill treatment you have known at my hands, I now make full amends. I have prospered in Florence, and shall share my prosperity with you. Come and find welcome with me.

This, from

Guaracco

I glared up as the cloaked figure lifted a hand to undo the mask.

The face of Lisa looked into mine with deep, dark eyes. "I have come to take you back to Florence," she said mechanically.

I was staring at her, and my eyes must have looked like the eyes of a frog. "What is the matter, Lisa?"

For something was the matter. She moved and

spoke as though in a dream. "I have come to take you to Florence," she said again.

Guaracco had done it, had put his spell upon her, and had sent her all the way to that perilous, besieged fortress to assure my own obedience to his call.

"Will you come?" she asked me, in such measured tones as she might have used to read from a book. Her eyes were upon me, drawing my gaze to them, but they only half knew me.

I could not refuse; Guaracco had been sure of that when he had sent Lisa after me in this bemused state. I felt rage and fear and confusion, but I could not send her back to him alone.

I flung my red mantle about me. "Come," I said to her.

We went ashore. Another familiar figure was on the dock, a tiny figure: Guaracco's ugly dwarf. "Our horses are ready at yonder hostler's," he greeted me. "Nay, I can answer no questions. My master will tell you all. Trust him."

Trust Guaracco! I did not know whether to laugh or to curse.

We rode swiftly away in the brightening morning, Lisa and the dwarf and I. The horses were good and I found mine easy to manage, for all I had not put foot in stirrup for six years. Lisa, too, controlled her mount, but she neither spoke to me nor looked at me. The dwarf led the way, hunched on his own beast like a trained monkey.

We took the road that once I had galloped with Lorenzo's officers. This time we paused once, at an inn where fresh horses awaited us. We changed to them, and took a cup of wine and some bread and cheese as we sat our saddles. Eventually, as sunset came luridly, we rode into the valley of the Arno, and as twilight grew gray, I saw Florence again, the city caught midway on the black and silver cord of the river, with gloomy fields all around.

As we came near, a gun sounded, and the dwarf grumbled that the watch would take its evening post at the gates. For my sake, he said, we must not enter by the highway. I might be recognized, for all the change in my appearance.

We turned, therefore, into the yard of a waterside house above the city, and our hideous little guide whispered to certain acquaintances of his. We left our horses and boarded a small open barge. It dropped downriver with us, drifted stealthily within the walls and under the bridges, and came at last to a wharf where we disembarked. Almost immediately at hand was a house I knew, the house where Guaracco once had offered me the gift of Lisa, where he and I had experimented and quarreled together, where now he must wait for me.

We walked along the street to the front door, and at the door we paused. I spoke to Lisa, but she made no reply.

"Knock," the dwarf said to me.

I did so, and divined the presence within of a
watcher. But there was no response, no audible movement even. It was only when Lisa, prompted in her
turn by our companion, spoke her name softly that
we heard a rattle of bars and the door opened a trifle.

There stood Guaracco's other dwarf, the handsome
one who acted as porter. He held in his hand a drawn
sword, and his eyes, turning up to me, were bright
and wary.

"Enter," he whispered. "They wait for you."

Again I tried to speak to Lisa, but she was walking
slowly around the side of the house. I stepped into
the front hall.

There stood a sizable oblong table, littered with
papers, and men sat in chairs along its sides. At the
head of the board stood Guaracco, as though he had
been addressing his companions. He did not seem
changed in so much as a red hair of his beard or a
gaunt line of his figure. He looked up and saw me,
cried out as if in joy, and strode quickly around the
table to me. Before I could move, he caught me in
his arms with a great appearance of affection.

"My cousin, my cousin!" he was saying, and his
grin was within six inches of my face. "You have
come, as I begged, to help me in the hour of my
triumph!"

His right arm, clasping my body, had slid under
my loosened mantle. It pressed something against my

side, something round and hard —the muzzle of a pistol. If I should move quickly, or speak to deny or denounce him, I would die on the instant.

That pistol-bearing hand urged me forward, as though he still embraced me in loving fashion. He led me to the head of the table and there held me beside him.

"Gentlemen, this is my kinsman Leo," he informed the company. "I have told you of him, and his wonders you have heard talk of in the past. He has more scientific miracles at his fingertips than all the saints in the calendar. And he has come to join us, from beyond the sea."

"I know him," said a thin, shifty-eyed man in black and crimson. "He was once pointed out to me at the palace. It was said that Lorenzo set great store by him."

"Are you then satisfied?" Guaracco asked the others. "With him as our helper, we cannot fail."

"If he is true to us —" began a square-faced man.

"I vouch for his loyalty," promised Guaracco, his gun prodding me.

Their silence gave him consent, and he went on:

"All is agreed, then. By this time tomorrow night we shall be in full possession of Florence, and ready to dictate to Tuscany as a whole. The oppressors will have shed their last drop of blood; the magistrates will speak and act only as we see fit to bid them."

"The people?" asked the square-faced man. He wore a leather riding tunic, and his eyes burned from under heavy black brows.

"The people will offer no trouble, even if we cannot rouse them, Captain Montesecco," replied Guaracco. "Did you not have charge of gathering two thousand hired soldiers outside the walls?"

"I had that charge, and fulfilled it," said the man called Montesecco. "And it is well we strike at once, ere so many armed men cause suspicion. Yet the Florentines are many and valiant."

"We can count on supporters among them," volunteered the man in black and crimson. "We Pazzi have servants and dependents to the total of several hundred. Our houses are close together in one quarter of the town, and a rising of our households will mean the rising of all that part of Florence."

As he mentioned his family name, I was able to identify him as Francesco Pazzi. He was one of a family of Florentine bankers, not so rich or powerful as the Medici, but ambitious and energetic.

"All of us stand ready save my cousin Guglielmo," he continued. "You, Messer Guaracco, advised against telling him of our plan."

Guaracco nodded his head. "Aye, he is married to Lorenzo's sister. Later, with his brothers-in-law out of the way, Messer Guglielmo will be glad to join us. But how of your uncle, Giacapo, the head of the family? What is his temper tonight?"

"I did not fetch him here, of course," said Francesco Pazzi, "for he clings to those archaic ideals of fair play. Howbeit, he knows that there is to be a rising against the Medici, whom he has ever hated as upstarts and thieves. He says he will lead the muster of our armed followers."

Another of the group at the table gave a quick little nod of approval. He was tall and high-shouldered, a scraggy-necked fellow in a purple gown, and he had a shallow, pinched jaw, like a trowel.

"What is my task?" he asked eagerly, as though fearful lest all the blood be spilt by other hands.

"A task worthy of Francesco Salviati of Pisa," Guaracco flattered him. "I rely upon your eloquence and courage. Either might suffice, and both will be invincible."

"You intend to assign him to the palace?" asked Pazzi.

"Aye, that," nodded Guaracco. "I shall send with you some of our best blades, Salviati. At the appointed time, you will lead them to the Palazzo Publico, where the magistrates will be sitting in judgment. Look, I will draw a diagram."

Dipping pen in ink, he began to sketch on a sheet of white paper for all to see. "Once up the stairs," he explained, "you come into a hall. There, ask the guard to summon the magistrate of the day. While the guard is gone to do so, let your men pass through this door which you will see upon your left hand."

He pointed with his pen. "It leads to an antechamber large enough to hold them all. When the magistrate arrives, you will tell him that liberty is at hand for Florence, and that he will be permitted to join us. If he refuses, call forth your band to teach him wisdom."

"And what of my assignment?" prompted yet another, one of three who sat together at Guaracco's right hand. He was youngish, hook-nosed and well dressed, but with a look about him of fine breeding gone slovenly. "I am a sure hand with a dagger," he boasted.

"I mind it well, Messer Bernardo Bandini," said Guaracco, smiling. "You and Messer Francesco Pazzi will strike down Giuliano de' Medici, and see that he does not rise again. Have I your approval?"

Bernardo Bandini grinned, and Guaracco turned his smile toward Captain Montesecco. "Our friend the captain promises to deal Lorenzo his death."

"If I miss stroke, may my sword arm wither," vowed the sturdy soldier.

"And as for my cousin Leo," went on Guaracco, fixing his eyes upon me, "whose wisdom and science are of such high quality, I will place him as our general in these various ventures."

Again he clapped me on the back, and I felt the pistol in his hand.

XIX. THE CONSPIRACY

Thus Guaracco planned a supreme stroke of ruthless and treacherous violence, and again he was dragging me into his service, to use my brains and skill as so often before. Even I, listening, saw how the scheme would succeed.

The strategy called not for a single blow but several, all struck at the same moment at the unsuspecting brothers Medici and their officers. Lorenzo and Giuliano would be assassinated. The Palazzo Publico would be seized, and the magistrates there taken into custody by armed men. The adherents of the plotters would rise in an impressive array, swaying the unprepared and perhaps dissatisfied citizenry by promises. And, to guard against the forming of a violent resistance, two thousand mercenaries were ready to march into Florence.

It could not fail. With the destruction of Lorenzo's power, my exile and danger would be past. Yet my first strong impulse was to cry out against so bloody a coup.

But if I spoke up, my life would be forfeit; I would not live to get out of the room. Therefore, I remained silent, while Captain Montesecco asked when and where the Medici brothers were to be struck down.

"Tomorrow morning," said Guaracco. "At church."

"Church?" repeated the captain sharply.

"Aye, that. Tomorrow is Easter Sunday, and we cannot be sure of getting them together at any other time. Young Cardinal Riario is to sing mass at the cathedral, which will insure their attendance. We will be ready for them, each nearest his man. At the moment when the host is elevated, and all attention is directed thither —"

"Nay!" cried Montesecco. He started from his chair, his black brows lifted into horrified arches. "I cannot draw sword at that holy moment. God would be watching me!"

Guaracco chuckled, and so did the trowel-jawed Francesco Salviati. But Montesecco was not to be laughed out of his impulse. "I have sworn to help," he said, "and I shall do so, or my name is not Giovanni Battista Montesecco. I will command the mercenaries, arrest the officials, help to rouse the city to our aid; but I cannot and will not do murder in the cathedral!"

"The man of blood shows himself bloodless," sneered Pazzi.

"Who says that?" flared the captain. "If you will take a sword in hand, Messer Francesco, and step outside for a short minute, you will end up more bloodless than I."

But Guaracco hurried to catch Montesecco's leather-clad shoulder in a big, placating hand. "None dare call you coward, Captain. Withdraw from that particular assignment if you will. None will blame you, and we can use your talents well elsewhere. Bernardo Bandini, are you still ready to deal with Giuliano?"

"Aye, that," replied Bandini heartily.

Guaracco's eyes shifted to the two men who had not yet spoken. Both were clad in black, and their faces were somber to match.

"What do you tell us, Antonio Maffei? Methinks you lived once in Volterra, which Lorenzo saw fit to sack and destroy."

Volterra . . . Guaracco had procured its destruction, primarily to get a crystal of alum for our unsuccessful time reflector. He had used the same infamy to get me out of the way when I might have been a stumbling block. He was able now to use the incident against Lorenzo.

"I am certain," said Antonio Maffei, with a growling relish, "that Lorenzo de' Medici's blood will smell sweet to the saints in heaven."

"He is a devil, and merits urging to hell," added Pazzi.

"Your gossip, Stefano da Bagnone there, will help

you," said Guaracco to Antonio Maffei. "You make a sign of assent, Messer Stefano, as I take it. And I may provide a third for your dagger party." Again he flicked his eyes at me. "But let us speak no more of it tonight, gentlemen. We shall meet early on the morrow, and then to work."

He let them out by a rear door. Francesco Pazzi, the last to go, he detained for a moment. "Keep an eye upon Captain Montesecco," warned Guaracco. "He has turned strangely squeamish for a professional killer."

"It shall be done," Pazzi assured him, and departed. Guaracco turned upon me with a sultry grin of welcome. "My boy," he cried, "fine things are to be our doing within the next twenty-four hours."

"Do you mean murder?" I flung at him. "Anarchy? Riot?"

"Surely you did not feel so harshly when Lisa —"

"Lisa, under your power of will, brought me here to you," I broke in. "I demand that you free her of your spell, and at once. She and I shall depart before another hour has passed."

"I think not," he said, in his familiar easy manner of mastery.

"Guaracco, I am vastly different from the young dupe you lyingly accused to Lorenzo. I am a killer, a desperate man. Bring on your dwarfs, and see if they can frighten me. I returned only to take Lisa from you, and by the saints, I shall do even so."

"Lisa?" he repeated. "Where is Lisa?"

And I realized that I did not know.

"Ah, cousin, I was beforehand with you. I hold her a hostage for your good will and support." He waved toward a chair. "Sit down."

Helplessly I obeyed him, and he talked.

The Pazzi, he said, were powerful but extravagant, and tottered on the verge of bankruptcy. They had agreed readily to work for him to the overthrow of the Medici, failing to understand that when the overthrowing was complete Guaracco need but bide his time to overthrow them also.

"Florence is as good as mine tonight," he said. "After Florence, I will take other states. All of Italy." He beckoned. "Come."

I followed him down some rough stairs to the cellar where we had worked together. It seemed stacked with firewood, until Guaracco kindled a lantern. Then I saw that the stacks were weapons.

These were guns—not clumsy arquebuses, but well-balanced rifles, with bayonets. There were boxes of grenades, and canisters that must hold high explosive. I thought I saw a machine gun. I turned a blankly wondering face toward Guaracco, and he laughed the old superior laugh.

"I quarried these weapons, or the knowledge to make them, from that bemused mind of yours, Leo. I had two years to delve into your trances, and six more to forge and fashion. What ordinary army could stand against me?"

"You have soldiers?"

"When first you came, you saw the worshippers I governed by tricks of false magic. These, and more like them, will rally at my call to use these arms. After that —but, Leo, you cannot demur longer. You and I need each other to succeed, indeed to exist."

He plunged ahead with an eloquent lecture upon his plans. After the subjugation of Italy, the subjugation of France and Spain, a united and submissive Europe would recognize Guaracco as its lord of lords. Cristoforo Colombo would be sought out, given his fleet, and sent to America to win its wealth.

"Once you spoke fancifully of such an empire," he reminded me. "Well, and am I not the true master sorcerer with whom all things come to pass?"

"Not all things," I mocked him. "I remember that I told the defeat for such a master —death. It will come to you, Guaracco."

He showed me his teeth. "Do not seek to kill me, lest you lose Lisa. Join me, and she is yours."

I made him no reply.

"If you turn your back on me, I may give her to Bernardo Bandini for stabbing Giuliano. Or I may use her to persuade that hesitant mercenary adventurer, Montesecco."

"You would not dare," I said slowly and bitterly.

"You know that I would. You can have Lisa only if you are my devoted lieutenant."

"She loves me," I said stoutly.

"That is because I bade her love you. My will can command her to love any man I choose."

I gazed at him as though I had never seen him before. I knew now that I must delay no longer. I must kill Guaracco, for the sake of Lisa and myself and all the world.

In one motion I bared my dagger and darted it at him.

He reeled back with a grunt, but no blood came. My point had turned against a concealed shirt of mail. He extended his arm, dangling the lantern above an open cask. "There is powder inside," he warned. "Attack me again, and you will force me to drop it."

I heard pattering feet. The two dwarfs were at me, with their drawn blades. But I kicked the hunchback and felled him, then sprang across him and darted upstairs.

"Lisa! Lisa!" I cried.

Only the roared curses of Guaracco answered me.

"You cannot catch me!" I yelled, on inspiration. "I will give myself up to the officers, go back to my prison!"

I reached the front door and ran out. Away I fled, past Verrocchio's *bottega*, around a corner to a broader street, and toward the heart of Florence. For I had only pretended that I was fleeing the city.

What now? Seek out Lorenzo and warn him? Would he believe me? Would he spare my life? Ahead of me loomed the Palazzo Publico, destined for a stirring scene at tomorrow's uprising. I had a sudden hope and plan.

Boldly I went to a side door and knocked. A porter opened to me.

"I am the locksmith," I said. "I am come to fix the door of the antechamber."

"I have heard of no orders," he argued, but let me enter and mount the stairs to the upper floor.

Here was a reception hall, and a door opening to the left. Guaracco had designated it as an ambush for the braves who would follow Francesco Salviati. I examined its heavy lock, and with my dagger made shift to drag it partially from the door. Still watched by the curious porter, I tinkered with its inner mechanism.

"Now it will serve," I told him, and went my way.

I had bent a spring and pried out a rivet. Any man or man, going into that antechamber and closing the door, would not get out again without the aid of a better locksmith than I.

After that, I sought a livery stable. In the pouch at my belt, given me aboard the ship on which I had escaped from the fortress, were some silver coins, and with them I hired a horse. Somehow, I wheedled my way past the watch at a gate and made the best time darkness would allow to the old familiar country house which Guaracco still kept.

A single caretaker opened to my thunderous knocking. Without ceremony, I drew my dagger and swore to cut out his liver if he opposed me by word or deed, then locked him in a closet. I took a lamp down to the cellar workshop where Guaracco had tested my scientific knowledge on our first day of acquaintance.

It was in a dusty turmoil, but in a corner among odds and ends of machinery was what I had hoped to find, the remains of our unsuccessful time reflector. I checked the battery. Though it was in bad shape, materials were at hand to freshen it. When I had restored it to power, I procured salt from the kitchen and mixed a great basin of brine. Finally I attached wires to the terminals of the battery, and thrust their ends into the liquid.

I watched carefully, hopefully. Electrolysis commenced. The bubbles that rose at the negative wire would be liberated hydrogen; those from the positive end were what I wanted.

I fetched from a shelf a glass bottle, holding more than half a gallon, filled it with brine and inverted it above this stream of bubbles from the negative wire. Slowly the gas crowded out the salt water, lying greenish-yellow in the bottle. I stoppered the bottle as it filled, then charged a second and a third container. Finally I drew the wires out. The bottles had earlike rings at their necks, and I strung them on a girdle under my cloak.

They were now a weapon for me that Guaracco had not dreamed of; for I had produced chlorine gas, such as had poisoned armies in the First World War, the war that was still centuries ahead of me.

As I finished the work, Sunday dawned grayly.

In the upper hall I found the sword that Giuliano de' Medici had given me, and slung it to my side. I released the frightened caretaker, and rode once more to Florence.

XX. APRIL 26, 1478

Il Duomo, Saint Mary's of the Flower, was the second cathedral in all Christendom. I was there, gas bottles and all, the next morning before Cardinal Riario began to sing mass.

I tried to lose myself among the throngs of worshippers who strolled most informally among the banks of seats in the octagonal choir beneath the great open dome. For once, I was glad of the natural darkness that clung in the cathedral, lighted only by the ornate upper windows.

At the high altar the cardinal, young and handsome for all his dignity, was intoning the service. I found a shadow beside a carved wooden screen, and tried to shrink my height by bowing my shoulders under my mantle.

More Florentines appeared, and more, brave in all the colors and fabrics of their rich Sabbath costume. A tall, ruddy head and beard showed among them —Guaracco, I saw at once. In my heart I prayed that he would fail to see me, and so he did. He was looking that day for other things, and perhaps he believed that I had indeed fled from Florence.

Then, on the other side of the choir, a flash of blue velvet, a smiling, handsome face. It was Giuliano de'

Medici, and his arm was linked in friendly fashion with that of Francesco Pazzi. On the other side of Giuliano walked Bernardo Bandini, the dissolute young man on whom Guaracco had threatened to bestow Lisa.

Then someone strolled past me at close quarters. It was Lorenzo, gorgeous in a crimson houppelande, sword at side, chatting with the crooked poet Agnolo Poliziano. Behind them, tense and pale, slunk the dark-clad figures of the assassins Maffei and Bagnone.

Almost I took a step toward the ruler of Florence. I drew in my breath to voice a warning, in the midst of that holy service. I saw Guaracco approaching beyond some chairs.

It was at that moment that the young cardinal's voice rang out with the words that, all unknowingly, set the cue for violence. *"Hoc est enim Corpus Meum!"* He genuflected, then arose and elevated the now consecrated host.

Maffei, the vengeful Volterran, was closer to me than Bagnone. He stepped suddenly forward, clutching at Lorenzo. His dagger twinkled in air.

I sprang, as though flung forward by a lever.

Had I been a true Florentine, I would have paused to draw sword, and that would have been too late to save Lorenzo. Being a Twentieth-Century American, I struck with my fist. Maffei staggered under the blow. His thrust, pushed out of line, glanced along Lorenzo's neck.

"Beware, Magnificence!" I cried, and struck Maffei again.

He had turned toward me, and my knuckles landed on the point of his chin. He sat down, suddenly and heavily, in a great flurry of black robes. I set my foot on his dagger hand. The weapon clanked on the floor, and I kicked it away.

All had become howling confusion. My gas, I saw, would affect not only Guaracco's party, but the whole congregation; I dared not release it. At last I thought to draw my sword.

Across the octagonal choir, chairs were overturning and horrified people scurried and gesticulated. Through the stir of motion, I saw Giuliano's blue-velvet clad body on the floor while Francesco Pazzi, with a knee on Giuliano's breast, struck and struck again with his dagger. Beyond them gleamed more drawn steel.

"Down with the Medici oppressors!" I heard Guaracco trumpeting.

A prolonged and many-voiced cheer answered him. Plainly the service had been liberally attended by supporters of the conspiracy. I spared a glance for the young cardinal; staring in horror, he shrank back from the altar, and a deacon tried to lead him away. Maffei had risen, but he ran before the menace of my sword-point. I looked to see what had happened to Lorenzo.

He had drawn his own sword and was parrying

the wild daggar thrusts of Bagnone, but his wound streamed blood and the terrified Poliziano hampered him by clinging to him.

I ran at them and thrust at Bagnone. My stroke was turned, for, like Guaracco the night before, Bagnone wore mail under his gown. Yet the hard-digging jab drove him back. I gestured Poliziano toward a doorway with my weapon.

"There is the sacristy!" I shouted. "Get him in there and bolt the door against these murderers!"

"Giuliano," Lorenzo was quavering. "Is Giuliano safe?"

But I gave him an unceremonious shove, and a moment later Poliziano had dragged him to the threshold of the sacristy.

"Down with the Medici!" Guaracco was yelling, close upon me. I faced around, and saw half a dozen of the conspirators rushing to cut Lorenzo off from escape. I threw myself in their way, engaging the blade of the foremost. Behind me the door of the sacristy clanged shut, and the bolt shot with a great ringing thump.

"Medici! Medici!" I roared, fencing with two men at once. "Murder! Help, honest men, murder is being done!"

"Medici!" someone echoed my cry, and never have I heard a more welcome voice.

A robust cavalier in plum-purple hurried to my side. He, too, held a sword, and struck manfully at the conspirators. His example fired others. In a trice the entire floor of the choir was a melee of jabbering voices and clashing steel.

Several armed guardsmen made their appearance. I saw Guaracco fleeing. I followed suit, for I remembered that Lorenzo, whose life I had just saved, thought me a criminal.

The public square outside the cathedral swarmed with people, some of them armed and angry, others frightened and mystified. All were talking at once, and nearly all were shouting: "Medici! Medici!" In this quarter of Florence, at least, the people were for their ruler.

A fellow in a jerkin of falding, with gray hair and a cast in his eye, stopped me with a fierce clutch even as I emerged from the door and ran down the steps. "Is it true that Giuliano de' Medici is slain?"

"I fear so," I replied. "I saw him struck down."

The gray head shook, but the man grinned. "Come to the Palazzo Publico, young sir," he invited me. "There is rare sport."

"What then?"

"Francesco Salviati and some cutthroats went up to seize the magistrates. But some of them were trapped in a room with a faulty lock."

Joy surged into me. My device had worked. "And what befell?"

"Some guards and other friends of the Medici came and captured the lot," replied the gray-haired man with relish. "Even now they are being hanged from a window sill, like hams from a rafter."

Brutal as it sounded, that news came gladly to my ears. Guaracco's conspiracy had failed in part at the cathedral; it had failed utterly at the palace. But I had no time for self-congratulation. Danger stalked elsewhere in Florence.

"Nay, come with me," I harangued my new friend. "I know of better sport still." I raised my voice. "Hark, all true Florentines and loyal servants of the Magnificent, who will fight for Lorenzo de' Medici?"

"I!" called a youth, brandishing a stout cudgel.

"And I!" roared another.

"I! I! I, too!"

Half a score crowded around me in as many seconds.

"Then follow," I said, and set off at a trot for the Pazzi quarter.

As I ran, I unslung from my belt two bottles of chlorine gas, and held one in each hand. The citizens set up a shout of enthusiasm or excitement, and a crowd of them hurried at my heels.

We had not far to run; out of a narrow side street rode a man on horseback—a man bright of eye and erect of body for all the whiteness of his hair. He wore gold-filigreed armor on chest and legs, and waved a sword. Armed footmen came at his heels.

"Liberty! Liberty!" He raised the war cry of the Pazzi. "Overthrow the oppressors!"

This must be Giacopo Pazzi, the aged but sturdy head of the rebellious family. Behind him were marshaled the retainers of his house, a good hundred of them. They carried swords and pikes, and they looked dangerous. Masses of the citizenry pressed from other streets to stare, perhaps to join.

There was nothing for it but audacity.

"*Medici!*" I thundered back at the horseman, and flourished one of my bottles as though it were a flag. "Forward, loyal Florentines! Smite these assassins!"

My own following set up a plucky shout, and pressed forward with me. I had more adherents than I had thought at first; perhaps we had been reinforced by others as we passed along the street. But Giacopo Pazzi was not the man to be daunted. He had come out looking for trouble, and he seemed glad to find it.

"Liberty!" he cried again, and spurred his horse to a trot, to ride me down.

Mounted, he could have scattered my band, for we were all afoot. But I hurled one of the bottles. It burst on the pavement several yards in front of the horse, which checked and pranced. I ran close and threw the second.

That smashed almost under the horse. The cloud of gas, rising and mixing with the air, must have driven sharply into Giacopo Pazzi's eyes and nose, as well as into the nostrils of his horse. The poor beast snorted and reared. Pazzi kept his seat with difficulty.

Coughing, he dropped his sword and put a hand to his throat. Next moment his frightened horse sidled into the foremost rank of his own men, throwing them into disorder.

The onlookers knew even less of what had happened than did Giacopo Pazzi, but they saw that he had lost command of the situation. Hoots and jeers rang in the air.

"Medici!" I screamed again.

"Medici! Medici!"

I hurried almost into the midst of the disorganized Pazzi party. From my belt I wrenched my third and last bottle of gas, and threw it.

It broke only a few feet from me, and the fumes momentarily blinded and strangled me as well as others. I retreated as best I might, coughing and dabbing at my tear-filled eyes. But even though I could scarcely see, I knew that that final dose of irritating gas had completed the job of halting the rush to dominate the city.

On all sides rose an increasing hubbub of loud shouts for the Medici, and then, as my vision cleared once more, I saw a flash of armor. Guardsmen were making their appearance, threatening the parade with swords and halberds. The foremost armed servants of the Pazzi faltered and drew back, crumpling the head of the column. Several darted away to right and left, losing themselves in the crowd.

Giacopo Pazzi had recovered somewhat from his

taste of chlorine. He was no coward, but he knew when he was beaten. He spurred quickly around a corner and away, before he could be reached and dragged from his saddle.

I thought, and indeed I hoped, that he might reach the gates and escape. To me, he seemed the least grisly of all that horde of unsavory plotters.

An officer of the guard passed close to me, and I hailed him. "How goes it in other places?"

"The rebels are all taken or slain," he answered. "His Magnificence is wounded, but he spoke from the balcony of the Palazzo Publico, begging that there be no more butchery of his enemies, and saying that the survivors will be given a fair trial. He urges peace, even while his tears stream for his dead brother."

"Nay, it is not over yet," I admonished him. "Keep watch on the gates. Some mercenaries have been gathered there to attack."

"We know that," he told me. "They will never enter the city."

I turned from him toward the Arno.

There was another thing to do, and it lay with me to do it.

XXI. THE LOVE OF LISA

Close by the river, Guaracco's house never looked so quiet and yet so forbidding. I ran to the door and tried it. From within, a voice challenged me cautiously.

"I am from Guaracco!" I called back. "All is lost in the city."

The door sagged open. With my shoulder I bore strongly against it, and it creaked back.

A cry of angry protest greeted me. The ugly dwarf swung up his curved sword, but my own point was quickly in his throat, and he fell dying. I hurried inside without waiting for him to cease his struggles.

"Lisa!" I shouted as I ran through room after room. "Lisa, my love, where are you?"

"Leo . . ."

It was muffled, little louder than a whisper, from somewhere beneath me. I found the stairs and ran down to the cellar.

Light gleamed there. Lisa sat upon a chest that must have been full of weapons. A lantern hung above her head. "Leo," she murmured, as softly as the sigh of wind heard far away. "You have come back."

"We will fly from here," I panted at her. "These

devil's machines and weapons shall be destroyed within the minute. And we are leaving Florence together, and forever, before Guaracco finds us."

"I must stay," she protested, as though she reminded me of the obvious. "I was told to wait."

"Aye, told by Guaracco," I said, for I knew that he had bound her to her place by hypnotism, stronger than shackles.

"He said that all would be well," murmured Lisa. "A new Florence, with no oppression —"

"Lies, lies!" I cried passionately. "He tried to form himself a kingdom of blood and evil, founded upon corpses." I caught her hand. "Lisa, come with me."

She rose to her feet, but it was like trying to lead a straw dummy. "I must wait, Leo."

I caught her by the shoulders, and tried to shake her into rationality. "Lisa, do you love me?" I pleaded. "Or is that only an illusion, too, turned on and off by Guaracco, like the spigot of a wine cask?"

"Love you?" Her eyes met mine at last, deep blue. Her lips trembled. "Yes. I love you."

That was definite enough. "Then we go from here."

I walked toward the stairs, drawing her with me, looking back into her eyes. She came a few steps, then stared past. Her eyes widened. Her mouth opened. "Beware, Leo!"

She tore from my grasp and fairly scurried around me, so that she was between me and the stairs. I turned on my heel, only swiftly enough to see what she had seen.

Guaracco had descended upon us. His hand was lifted, holding something that gleamed. I heard the bark of an explosion, saw a sudden ghostly puff of smoke. And Lisa sagged against me, into my arms.

Her eyes were suddenly bright and wakeful again. Her mouth trembled into a smile. As I eased her body to the floor, it slackened in my arms. I knew that she was dead.

"Do not move, Leo."

Still at the foot of the stairs, Guaracco leveled his weapon at me. "This fires six shots. It is one of the guns I made according to the science I learned from you."

His thumb had drawn up the hammer of the revolver, and the muzzle stared me between the eyes. I knelt beside Lisa and waited. I did not fear to die; I only feared that Guaracco might live. "You have failed," I told him.

"Failed?"

"Lisa was under your spell, but she broke it to save my life." I rose to my feet. "She loved me. Her love was more than all your dirty conjuring tricks."

He actually smiled. "I am glad that she did save you. Leo, we must not fight each other. There is still time and opportunity for us to help each other escape and live."

I shook my head without speaking.

"Many have died today," went on Guaracco. "Why should we? If you cannot understand, look also at this."

His free left hand extended toward me. Between thumb and forefinger shone a globule of rosy-silver light. "It is the pearl of sleep, Leo. Look upon it."

I looked. I felt my senses sway, but I held them firm. It was only a pearl. The light did not wax or blur or brighten; I was resisting his spell. It was only a pearl there in Guaracco's hand. He tried to trap me with it, but he could not. I stared, and I would not let it take the mastery of me.

"You are going to sleep, Leo," Guaracco was intoning. "To sleep. And all is well between us."

My mind worked furiously. A way opened to revenge, if I could but be cunning. Slowly, stiffly, I made a step toward him. He thought himself the winner.

"Leo, Leo," he droned, "I am your friend. I am Guaracco, who adopted you as his cousin, who made you great and wealthy. You will be grateful, Leo. You will help Guaracco."

Slowly, as in a trance, I took another step.

"You will be grateful, Leo. You will tell Lorenzo de' Medici that Guaracco, too, fought to put down the conspiracy. Those who can say otherwise are dead now."

It would have worked, that plan. I let him deceive himself, and made a third slow step. We were almost within reach of each other. The revolver in his right hand was bigger and brighter than the pearl in his left. I kept my face gravely rapt, my eyes staring.

"Lorenzo will believe us and reward us," Guaracco insisted. "Then we can work on together, plan again, more wisely. Together we can rule the world—"

I threw myself upon him.

He pulled the trigger, but my left hand was upon the revolver. Pain bit my thumb, where the firing pin drove deep into the base of the nail. I wrenched the weapon away and flung it behind me. It exploded with the shock, and the bullet sang into a beam overhead.

I hurled him staggering across the floor, and we both drew our swords.

"You triple traitor!" howled Guaracco, as I lunged at him. "Come, if you will have death this way!"

I made no reply, but deflected his riposte — another thing he had learned from me. His chest was exposed for a moment, but I knew that mail defended it, and swept my blade in a quick arc. He whipped his brow out of the way with millimeters to spare.

Running toward an open box, he tried to clutch a pistol out of it. I got there as soon as he, nicked at his outflung hand and got home. He whimpered; two of his fingers were shorn away, and blood fountained forth.

"Hold, Leo." He suddenly changed his tune. "I must not die, not if you hope to live, and —"

I did not hope to live, and made him no answer. I beat his sword aside and slashed at his face. His cheek was laid open, and his beard suddenly gleamed a deeper red.

"The time reflector," he was yammering at me. "Only I can show you how to rebuild and improve it, how to get back to your own age!"

He should have saved his breath, for he panted and choked. His thrusts were unsteady, easy to foil. A dig at his mailed belly drove most of the wind out of him, and drove out the fight as well. He tried to retreat to the stairs, but misjudged and brought his back against the blank-faced wall. He flung down his sword and lifted his hands. "Mercy, Leo! I surrender!"

His unwounded right palm spread itself against a stout timber. I darted my point at it, all my weight behind. My sword pierced his hand, and broke off. A tremulous, unmanned howl from Guaracco —his hand was spiked to the wood by my broken blade, like a big pale spider on a bodkin.

I flung down my hilt and stepped back. I spared no eye to my enemy's plight, nor ear to his prayers.

Lisa lay still and misty pale, but there was no blood on her calm face. I knelt and closed her eyes, straightened her body, drew her hands together and folded them upon her quiet breast. In her last instant of life, her mouth had fallen into the little close-lipped smile I had known.

Stooping almost to earth, I kissed her once. Her face was still warm.

"Leo, Leo, what will you do with me?" sobbed Guaracco in shameless entreaty.

He dabbed with his half-severed left hand at the broken blade that held him to the wood, but the point was wedged too tightly for him to pull free. "What will you do?" he asked again.

I let my actions answer him. From its peg I snatched the lantern. With my foot I stirred some straw and rubbish together into a mass against the foot of a barrel. He saw what I intended. "There is gunpowder in that barrel!" he shrieked.

I knew it, but still I spoke no word. With all my strength I dashed the lantern down. The glass shattered, the straw blazed up. And then I raced for the steps, and up them. Behind me fire gushed into a lurid blaze.

At the door of the house I almost trampled upon Guaracco's remaining dwarf, the handsomer one. He stared at me in mute horror, then at the glow behind me. He seemed to read in my face what had happened, for he went scuttling past me and dived into the flaming cellar as into a swimming pool.

"Master, Master!" he screamed.

I gained the street, ran along it for a score of paces

before the whole world seemed to burst into thunder and lightning. I was flung to my face, skinning my cheek on the pavement, but I rose and ran on. Behind me echoed another explosion and another.

That was the end of Guaracco's house, and his weapons and his dwarfs; the end of Guaracco himself, and of Lisa.

There remained nothing for me to do save to go and give myself up to Lorenzo.

XXII. THE CHRISTENING

In the evening I stood in the groined, frescoed chamber where first the ruler of Florence had given me audience.

Lorenzo de' Medici had sent away his clerk and his guards, and sat in his chair of state, behind the ebony and ivory table. His collar hung loose over the swaddle of bandages on his gashed neck, but otherwise he was the same Lorenzo I had always known—alert, self-contained, far-thinking.

"I am driven to believe all points of your strange story," he said gently. "Without fully understanding, I believe. No one can deny," he went on, "that you have saved Florence and me. So says Poliziano, and the officers of the guard. I grant you full pardon, and I ask you to pardon me for driving you away by my misjudgment. It shall not happen again."

I bowed, and thought only of Lisa. He was able to read my mind.

"Sorrow touches you," he said, "as it has touched me. You mourn your sweetheart as I mourn my brother."

"I cannot forget her, Magnificence."

"Do not forget her, but be comforted. Work will

help you, and me, too. Florence has need of my rule and your science."

"You are right," I agreed.

"Yours will be a great laboratory," he promised. "Aye, and a great studio will be yours, too, in the gardens of San Marco. Above all, I promise you honor and safety. But," and his hand drummed the ebony table-top, "one chief change is necessary."

"And that?"

"This matter of your strange journey to our age from another."

"You said you believed, Magnificence."

"Aye, but it must remain a secret between us. Others might think you were a devil's apostle, and urge that you be borne to the stake."

"True," I agreed.

"But, since the death of Guaracco and your lady Lisa, you and I alone know the story. Therefore, it is expedient that we provide you with an ordinary birth and family among us; a father, and all the rest."

"A father?" I echoed him, not comprehending.

"Aye, that. I know the very man—a notary who is in my confidence, who has several children already. He will gladly own you as yet another son, if I ask it of him. The records can be arranged in various offices to make it believable. Forget, then, that barbarous unpronounceable surname of yours." He smiled. "The name of the notary, your new father, is Piero da Vinci."

I sank down upon a chair, implications rushing upon me like waves of an incoming tide.

"Leave all arrangements to me," said Lorenzo. "It is one of my talents to make perfect all such little things." His bitterly ugly face grew suddenly beautiful with that warm smile of his. "From this day forward, I shall call you Leo —no —Leonardo."

He said it, and what he said in Florence was so.

And I knew the rich life given me to lead, as crown of the age and inspiration of ages to come.

My scientific gropings will show the way to doctors, engineers, philosophers. My paintings will dazzle nations. Michelangelo will hate me too much, and Raphael admire me too much, but both will be better for my examples.

Of my greatest paintings, the Last Supper will shine out its lesson of faith and hope, and to Judas I shall give the face of Guaracco; and that painting I shall surpass with one greater still, with La Gioconda named as model to be sure, but preserving the smile and spirit of Lisa —Mona Lisa. And I shall die old and great, with a king to weep for me.

I am Leonardo da Vinci.